Murder in Woods

AN AMATEUR SLEUTH MYSTERY

CELIA HARRISON

This is a work of fiction. Names, characters, places, events, and organizations are the author's imagination or are used fictitiously. Any resemblance to actual persons, live or dead, businesses, events, locales, or organizations is entirely coincidental.

Text copyright © 2024 by Ocean Light Publishing
All rights reserved.
No part of this book may be reproduced, copied, or transmitted in any form or by any means, without direct written permission from the author or the publisher. The only exception is for brief quotations used in reviews or promotions.

Prologue

Dear Diary,

Ben asked to see me, which I find strange because he doesn't need to ask to see me. I think he has a surprise. He's always filled with surprises. That must be why he's been acting strange lately.

The guys have decided to use this summer break to go on a trip, but I am not going. I'm not sure if I want to spend two weeks deep in the woods of Oregon, where there are mosquitoes and... actually, the mosquitoes are enough to keep me away. Madelyn isn't happy that I am not going, and she doesn't fail to remind me every day. She hasn't cooked breakfast for me for days, just to punish me.

Anyways, I have to decide on something nice to wear. The last time Ben and I went out, he had taken me somewhere fancy, but I wasn't dressed for that.

Later, I don't want to keep Ben waiting.

"You and Ben have another date?" Madelyn lay on my bed, her body in a star shape. She was my best friend and a fellow student here at Stanford. "Once more, my best friend abandons me for her boyfriend. The painful life a single woman like me has to go through."

"Don't be silly," I said, laughing. "I've been with you all day, and besides, I haven't seen Ben for days..." I turned to look at myself in the mirror. "He's been acting a bit strange lately."

"What do you mean?" She asked.

I shrugged. "I don't know," I said, letting my hair down as I reached out for a comb. I kept my hair down because Ben loved running his hands through it. He said I should flaunt it around rather than leave it in a tight bun. "I'll ask him about it today." I turned to look back at Madelyn. She was sitting up now.

"You said he texted, right?" She asked. "After two days, all he could send was a text?"

I nodded. "I brought it up, but he said he was with friends, and he couldn't hear me over the noise...Why do you ask?"

She shrugged. "Never mind. I must be reading too much into it. But after two days, the least he could do was come over, not send you a simple text."

I was worried now. "You think he was lying?"

"I know he was lying," she said. "But, don't worry about it. I mean, it's Ben we're talking about. The guy is crazy about you." It seemed she was going to say something, but she fell back on my bed.

Usually, Ben and I planned our date a few days beforehand, but this one had come on short notice. I looked down at my new dress. It was a gown I bought the last time

Madelyn and I went shopping. It was blood red and stopped just above my knees. "Is the dress revealing too much?" I asked her.

"Are you kidding? Dressed in that, you're going to kill Ben before his time." She giggled. I rolled my eyes and grabbed my jacket. "Come on, don't wear the jacket," she whined.

"It's cold out there."

"Good luck. Also, get me a big bucket of fried chicken on your way back. When I'm back from the cinema with the guys, I can have that for dinner."

I frowned. "I thought you were on a diet?"

"Not anymore. It's just a little weight. It can't kill me."

"That's what I told you. I can't see the weight you said you added. You're skinny to me."

"Wear your glasses, Amelia." She said and turned to face the wall.

I chuckled. Just then, my phone beeped, signaling a text came in. Ben was waiting downstairs. "I have to go."

"Ok, have fun."

The moment I saw Ben, I regretted wearing the gown. Ben was dressed casually. I, on the other hand... Luckily my jacket helped. He laid a chaste kiss on my lips. "How have you been?"

I ignored his question. "I should be asking you that," I said while getting into the car. "I haven't seen you for days." I waited for him to get in the car before I continued. "Are you ok?"

He smiled at me. "You look beautiful."

I felt my cheeks warming up at the compliment. "Thank you. Is something bothering you?"

He shook his head. "Nothing. I just...I just want to talk." I was worried now because his palms were shaking.

I bit my lips nervously. "Talk?"

"Yeah."

***

Thirty minutes later, I was back on my bed. Madelyn had gone to the cinema with Heather and Josh. I reached out for my diary.

Dear Diary,
Ben and I broke up.

Chapter 1

I hadn't believed in the whole 'happily ever after.' That's probably because I didn't see a completely happy couple. When Ben came into my life, I had held a tinge of hope in my heart. He wasn't perfect, and neither was our relationship. But we were happy—at least I was, till he decided to end our nine-month relationship. The question of where things had gone wrong started to rise. Why don't couples realize when their relationship takes the wrong road, so they can reverse course before falling off a cliff? I blamed myself for not seeing things clearer and letting my guard down.

"You should come with us," Madelyn said to me one day. "You can't keep moping around forever. It's been two weeks already." She stood before my bed, staring down at me. She had her hands on her waist, a pitiful look on her face.

"No. I'll stay here," I told her, burrowing deeper into my pillows. "And I don't care about Ben anymore," I added, which was a lie. "I've moved on." I dragged my pillows closer to my chest.

She sighed, taking a seat on my bed. "Please come with us, Amelia. It's summertime. I'll feel awful if we're out there having fun and you're here all by yourself." When I remained silent, she continued. "This trip will help take your mind off Ben," she added, brushing her fingers softly through my hair.

Madelyn was right. I needed to get my mind away from Ben, and I didn't want her to worry about me when she was supposed to be relaxing and having fun. So, I gave a bright smile. "You're right. I do need this vacation."

"Exactly, I'll call Josh and Heather and let them know you are coming!" Madelyn jumped up from my bed. I nodded and went back to my journal. Josh and Heather were both from my hometown. We had attended the same high school. Back then, though Josh and I were close, Heather and I hardly spoke. She was on the cheerleading team and was always with her team. It was here in Stanford when I ran into her that we got to talking.

Dear Diary,

I wrote slowly.

It's been two weeks since the breakup. Today, I finally gave in to go on the trip with the guys.

Although I told Madelyn that I had moved on, that was a big lie. I still have feelings for Ben. Nine months isn't nine days or weeks. It's almost a year. I can't just forget about him like he is an ant on the sidewalk. I need time to heal, and I need a good distraction. That's what this trip has to offer.

When I closed my journal that day, it hit me. Maybe Ben and I never turned to the wrong road. Maybe we had been on the wrong road right from the start.

***

"Did you hear?" Josh said, brushing back his auburn hair from his face. We had all gone out for lunch to talk about our coming trip. Now that I had decided to go, I started to look forward to it. We were going to stay at a cabin owned by Josh's family somewhere deep in the woods of Oregon.

"What?" Madelyn asked, looking at him. "Did someone die?" She raised her coffee to take a sip. Madelyn and Josh were the cat and rat of our group, and you could always trust them to start their silly bants.

He raised an eyebrow. "Why are your thoughts always revolving around the dark side?" With her sometimes sassy character, Madelyn had a baby-like face. She had her red hair packed behind today. She rolled her eyes and shrugged.

I laughed. "Don't mind her, Josh. What's up?"

"They finally found the—"

"Look, Heather has arrived." I pointed out as Heather strolled into the restaurant, her curls bouncing with each step she took, a bright smile on her face. Heather was a ray of sunshine, always brightening up the room with her presence.

"Hey guys, so I've got news," she said the moment she took her seat. She was breathing heavily like she had been running. Before we could ask any question, she continued,

"Uh...about the trip, is it okay if—" She choked, hitting her chest.

"Heather," Josh said, offering her water while I patted her back. "Try to relax before you speak."

"Yeah," she rubbed her throat, blinking away the tears that had gathered in her eyes. "Imagine if I died, what would be on my tombstone? Died from her own spittle," She said the last part in a dramatic tone. "Anyways, I was going to say—"

"You aren't canceling on us, right?" Josh was quick to ask. "You can't, not now."

"What? No. It's nothing like that," she said. "But a few of my friends would like to join us. I want to ask if you guys are OK with it," she said with a nervous grin, her eyes moving from me to Josh, then Madelyn.

I frowned. I had thought the trip was just going to be the four of us. I looked at Madelyn and Josh, but they already had big smiles on their face. I wasn't surprised that Josh was going to agree. He loved making new friends, just like Heather, but Madelyn surprised me.

Josh sighed. "Oh, good. I thought you were bailing on us. We just got Amelia to come on board," He told her, glancing at me. "We don't need someone backing out."

"These friends you talk about, do we know them?" I asked.

"No." She said, shaking her head. "I don't think so. They are two couples, by the way."

"Two couples?" I looked at the others. "That's four people. Is the cabin big enough?"

Heather gave a nervous laugh. "Is it too much? They heard about the trip and asked to join. I couldn't refuse, but I said I would ask you guys first." Heather had a problem refusing people.

"It's fine," Josh said with a shrug. "The more, the merrier. Who wouldn't love to make new friends?" Madelyn nodded in agreement.

"Amelia, are you cool with this?" Heather asked, seeming to notice I didn't look so happy about the idea.

I smiled at her. "Yeah, it will be fun. The more, the merrier," I said, stealing Josh's line.

Chapter 2

"So, I guess you're not pregnant then?"

I laughed. "No, Grandma, I'm not pregnant." I had gone to visit my parents, and also to inform Grandma about the trip. "You should check the friends you hang out with. It seems they do nothing but spread rumors about Alex and me."

"Yeah," my brother said.

Grandma laughed. "Please, those fowls aren't my friends. The only reason I hang out at the club is that chef Martin cooks for them, and his food is just heaven on Earth. You guys remember Angie?" She asked.

"The one that got that breast enlargement stuff?" Alex asked.

"No," she shook her head. "That's Bridget. Angie is the one that was caught sleeping with her husband's driver, and might I add, that's her third husband, another divorce in the bag."

"Amelia!" My mum shouted my name from the kitchen. "Come help me set the table. Lunch is ready."

Soon, we were sitting in the dining room eating food that...could have been better. I didn't voice this though, nobody dared. My dad always did the cooking in the house because before he married my mum, she didn't even know how to boil an egg. She started visiting the kitchen after she took early retirement from the bank. Although she had improved her cooking significantly, there was always room for improvement.

"How's the chicken?" Mum asked. "I used the spice you suggested, Marie," she said to my grandma. "Thanks for the tips, by the way."

"You're welcome," grandma told her with a smile. She was my mother's number-one hype woman. "And yes, it did bring taste to the chicken this time." Grandma was right. It did bring taste, a little too much, though.

"So Amelia," Dad said. "How are things going with that boyfriend of yours, Ben? I haven't seen him for a while now. Is he still preparing for exams?"

My parents didn't know Ben and I had broken up. I looked at Alex, who was looking back at me. Alex was the first person I told that night. I didn't want to call Madelyn since she was at the cinema, and my brother had called me by mistake. "Uh...No, he's done with his exams. He's been pretty busy. That's why." I told them, hoping they would move on to another topic.

"Maybe when you're back from the trip, you bring him over," my mum said. "I would love for him to try out my cooking." She gave a cheeky smile.

I decided to come out. "Mum, Ben and I broke up two weeks ago." I dropped my head.

"What?" Her spoon dropped to the table. "Are you serious?"

"Yeah." I shrugged. "It's nothing. Let's just drop the topic and talk about your chicken, which I must add, is really, *really* good. Great job, mum."

"Darling," My dad said, his voice soft. Now, they were going to start pitying me. "It's been two weeks? Why didn't you tell us?"

I didn't know what to say. I just wanted the spotlight away from me. "I told Alex." I found myself saying. He shot me a look, but I ignored him, bringing the chicken up to my lips but not taking a bite.

"And you didn't tell me." Grandma turned to Alex, a betrayed look on her face. Good, the attention was away from me.

"But Amelia didn't want me to," he said. "I couldn't go against her wish, especially not over something like that."

"He is telling the truth," I admitted. "I wanted to tell you myself. It's one of the reasons I came over. I didn't want to tell you over the phone."

"Well, honey, how are you feeling?" My mother asked.

"Great." I put up my brightest smile. I sighed, looking down at my food. "I am fine, really. I mean, it's been two weeks. By the time I'm back from the trip, I would have had so much fun, and I wouldn't even remember his name."

"A fowl, that's who he is," Grandma said. "A stupid fowl for letting you go. Someday, he's going to realize his mistake and come to you on his knees, begging for mercy."

Great advice, Grandma.

"Yeah," Alex nodded his head. "And besides, you guys shouldn't make it look like the end of the world," He said. "Amelia is young. There are other guys out there. Better and richer, and they probably know cute girls that Amelia could set me on a date with." I rolled my eyes.

"Yeah, but Ben was Amelia's first boyfriend," Mum said. "Surely—" she stopped. "You know what, Amelia doesn't want us to dwell much on this subject, so we'll pass it."

"Thank you," I muttered, dropping the chicken I had been holding in my hands. I reached for a tissue to clean the sauce that had stuck to my skin.

***

"How is everybody back home?" Madelyn asked when I entered the room. She was watching some cartoon, dressed in an oversized sweater and long stockings.

"Good," I replied.

She turned to face me. Her hand, which was full of popcorn, froze in the air just before her mouth. "What's wrong? You're not smiling." She dropped the popcorn back on the bowl that sat on her lap.

"Nothing. I just told my parents about the break-up." I collapsed on the chair, resting back. "My grandma called Ben a fowl."

She laughed. "Of course, I love your grandma."

"Yeah," I muttered. "Now that I've told them, that's one load off my head."

She nodded, watching me. "How are you feeling?"

I was going to tell her I was fine, but my body didn't agree with me. "My head hurts, my feet are in pain, and my stomach is begging for mercy."

"Your stomach? Are you on your period?" I shook my head. "What did you eat?" She asked.

"My mum cooked lunch." I pouted.

"I see. Oh, Heather asks that we meet her at the cafe tomorrow." Madelyn said.

"To hang out?" I was planning to have a long relationship with my bed tomorrow.

Madelyn shrugged. "I don't know. If you're hungry, I prepared dinner." She turned back to watch her cartoon.

I could feel my tummy give a little jump at her words. "Awww, so you're back to cooking for me." I hugged, rubbing my head on her shoulders.

"Don't feel special." She pushed me away.

Chapter 3

The days went by slowly. I found myself hiding in shadows with each day that passed. I felt that everyone was looking at me whenever I walked outside. It didn't help that Ben was around the campus. I always went out with a hoodie and dark shades to the disappointment of Madelyn, just to avoid being seen.

"You look ridiculous," she said as we entered the café. "There is no chance that you'll see Ben here. No one is looking at you—but your appearance is sure to attract attention." It was one of those situations where you would think everyone was looking at you and judging, but in reality, people were so busy you were not even the last thing on their minds. I knew that, but still.

I shook my head stubbornly. "I'm only trying to avoid an awkward meeting. What would I say to him if we came across?"

"Hey, Ben," she said in a fake Australian accent. "You look rather ravishing today. Since you broke my heart, eating you would be suicide." Madelyn winked.

"It's not funny, Madelyn. This is probably why you were kicked out of drama club." She had joined the drama club so she could audition and get the role of Raulet, a young peasant girl who ended up marrying Alfonso, a farmer, choosing him over the wealth of a prince who had been after her. Madelyn had wanted to get the role because she had a crush on the guy who played the role of Alfonso. In the end, we didn't go to see the play even after I bought tickets because Madelyn could not bear to see someone else kiss her Alfonso.

"Please." She rolled her eyes. "Those chipmunks don't know true talent when they see it. It was their loss anyway." I laughed, deciding to pull my hoodies off, but Madelyn was already reaching out. She raised the glasses off my nose, bringing them up to rest on my hair instead.

"Better," she said. "Now, you look like someone I want to hang out with." I pushed her gently. We sat beside the window to get a view of the outside. "I can see some color on your cheeks, no bags beneath your eyes, and a smile I see growing on your face."

I gave a small smile. "I'm moving on."

"Great, soon you'll forget about him totally," she assured. "Trust me. This might be your first heartbreak. I've gone through quite a number, and look at me, in a happy relationship." She flicked imaginary hairs off her shoulders.

I raised an eyebrow in question. "Madelyn, you're single. What 'happy relationship' are you talking about?"

She scoffed. "Excuse you, but I'm in a happy relationship with myself. I take myself out to dinner, buy myself flowers, and profess love to myself every day. I'm having the best relationship ever."

"Oh wow, you're such an amazing boyfriend."

"I know, right?" She blew on her fingers. "Anyways—fuck." Her eyes widened as she stared at something behind me. "Speak of the devil."

"What?" Out of curiosity, I tried to turn back, but she stopped me.

"Don't look back. Ben just walked inside."

My insides froze, my muscles going stiff. "Ben?"

"He's with some friends. Hold on. I think they are heading upstairs. They aren't looking this way. Once they go, we can leave if you want." She looked out the window, trying to hide her face. If Ben saw Madelyn, he knew I would be there.

I tried to catch him from the corner of my eyes as he passed. He looked good—he was laughing with his friends as they headed to the stairs. He put on his favorite sweater. Memories flashed through my eyes as I remembered wearing that same clothing a few times. His hair was longer now. He had it packed in a ponytail, though a lock of hair escaped and was over his face. A friend whispered something to him, making him laugh out loud. He looked happy—very happy. Soon, he was gone. He hadn't noticed me at the corner, watching.

"The asshole," I heard Madelyn mutter.

Ben wasn't a bad guy. When he said he felt our relationship was going down, he was willing to go on to see if we could get back on the right track. When did we ever get on the wrong track? I had asked him. He said he had been thinking of breaking up with me for a while but didn't want to hurt my feelings. I ended things there, and then. I wasn't going to make anyone feel trapped in a relationship. It hurt that he looked happier than when he was with me.

I turned to Madelyn with a smile. "It's nothing. He's allowed to be happy." But deep down, I didn't want him to be. I wanted him to be as down as I was. I wanted him not to be able to sleep at night, thinking of me. I wanted him to regret ever saying the words that led to our separation, just for him to be in my shoes for a while.

"You're also allowed to be happy," she said.

I nodded my head. "I know."

Soon, Heather arrived. There were two young ladies with her. One was a brunette who had a sweet smile on her face. Her hair was packed in two ponytails. There was something about her that reminded me of Heather. They gave off similar vibes.

The other girl wore a stylish tulle dress. She had her blonde hair twisted in curls.

"Hey," Heather greeted, taking a seat beside me. The brunette followed. I had to move closer to the window so that the chair could contain three people. The blonde sat beside Madelyn, facing us.

"Hi," Madelyn said in a loud voice, obviously surprised by the people Heather had brought.

"This is Daphne," Heather said, referring to the brunette. "And that's Lily." The blonde gave a small wave when she heard her name. "They are the ones I was telling you about.

I thought it would be better if you guys met before the trip. Lily graduated last year. She and I overlapped on the cheerleading team. Daphne works at the university bookstore."

"Hi," Madelyn turned to the girls. "I'm Madelyn, and this is Amelia."

"Nice to meet you," The girl named Lily said while brushing away some curls that had come over her face. I noticed the ring on her middle finger. I didn't know much about diamond rings, but it looked very expensive. "My husband and I would like some away time."

"Your husband? Heather didn't mention that you were married." I remembered that she said they were a couple, but I hadn't thought of marriage.

She smiled. "Newly wedded," she said, showing off her ring. "We just came back from our honeymoon. We had it in Paris." She looked at Daphne. "Daphne was the one who introduced Tom and me, so I'll forever thank her for my happy union."

Daphne shrugged. "After Lily and I met at a yoga class, I just knew she would be a perfect match with Tom. Lily just went through a breakup, and Tom also. When they met, it was an instant click."

"That's so sweet," Madelyn said. "Can you find a partner for me? I'm tired of being single." We all laughed at that.

"Sure," Daphne said. "How do you like them?"

"Young, rich, and handsome." I rolled my eyes at Madelyn's words. "Oh, and throw in a little bit of good personality and a sense of humor, with likable future in-laws."

We spent hours in the restaurant arguing and talking about our high school and college experiences, all the fun things girls loved to talk about.

"I should get going, Heather," Lily said. "Tom and I have an appointment with my lawyer. Remember?" Heather nodded. "Daphne, can you please give me a ride? I've texted Kelvin, but since he's with his sick wife at home." Daphne nodded. They both got up, said their goodbyes, and left.

"Who is Kelvin?" Madelyn asked Heather the moment the two girls left the cafe.

"Lily's personal driver."

"She has a personal driver?" Madelyn said in disbelief. "Is it too late to be a lesbian and marry her?"

If I were close to her, I would have landed her a smack. "You're a lost cause, Madelyn." I turned to Heather. "What's up with the lawyer?"

"Lily and Tom are planning on getting a joint-owned property? I wasn't really listening when she mentioned it."

"Really?" I was surprised. "Couples still do that?"

"Yeah," Madelyn said. "My parents did something like that after their marriage. The advantage is that if one dies, your partner earns everything. That's some true love stuff, I tell you. There has to be complete trust between my partner and me before I'm even willing to do something like that."

True love?

After a breakup, I wasn't ready to discuss about 'true love' or any kind of love.

Chapter 4

Dear Diary,
It's been three weeks since the breakup. I saw Ben the other day. He looked really happy. It hurt because I would think I wasn't the only one hurting, but it appeared he had moved on pretty fast. It did awaken something in me—reality. Maybe the fact that life isn't fair to everyone is what makes it fair, feeding humans from the same spoon.
Today is the day we leave. I'm excited about the trip.

I didn't have the best sleep. Madelyn woke me up as early as eight. "Isn't it too early?" I asked.

"Too early?" She exclaimed. "It's a seven-hour drive. You need to get up."

I got up when she threatened to pour me water. "You just don't know good sleep, Madelyn." She rolled her eyes and walked away to continue with her preparation.

One hour later, we were loading our things. "Amelia, come help me with my bag. This thing weighs a ton," Madelyn complained as she struggled to place her bag in the back of my old Ford Explorer. The car had belonged to my father, who handed it over to me when I had gotten accepted into Stanford. "What the hell did I pack in here?" I heard her say.

Unknown to Madelyn, I had put a few of my books in her bag when I ran out of space in mine. I knew she would never allow it. That's why I waited for her to get in the bathroom before setting into action. "Well, you were always a heavy traveler," I joked. "I'm busy over here. Go get Josh to help." I waved her away.

"Josh!" She shouted at the top of her voice.

"I heard my name," Josh said, approaching from behind. "Will it kill you if, when you call me, you don't yell for the whole world?"

She gasped. "Now, why would I want to do something that wouldn't annoy you?"

"Please, don't start one of your silly fights now," I pleaded.

"Josh, please help Madelyn," Heather said. "Her bones are getting tired nowadays. Old age is taking its toll."

"Fuck you, Heather," Madelyn cussed while we all laughed. Josh went over to help her.

"This isn't even that heavy, Madelyn." He picked up her bag with one hand.

"It is heavy!" Madelyn complained. "You just don't know because of those scary muscles you pack." She crossed her arms before her, letting out a huff. "Let's trade hands for a while. You'll see."

Josh dropped her bags at the back of the car. "Heather, when are your friends arriving?" Josh asked. We weren't carrying much load and had decided that we would buy most of the things we needed from any convenient store when we arrived in Oregon. "We have to leave now if we want to get there before nightfall."

Heather glanced down at her Apple Watch. "They should be here soon. I spoke with Anthony earlier. They are on their way."

"Which one is Anthony?" I asked, not sure if Lily's husband was Tom or Anthony.

"He's Daphne's boyfriend." I nodded and headed back to the apartment to get my last bag. It mainly contained underwear and pajamas, so it was the smallest one. When I came back, I saw Lily and Daphne had arrived.

Daphne stood with her boyfriend. Anthony was tall, muscular, and handsome. He looked like he was catapulted straight out of a Harlequin novel. Daphne smiled when she saw me. "Hi, Amelia. Meet Anthony, my boyfriend," she introduced.

I dropped my bags, stepping forward for a handshake. "Hi, nice to meet you." He accepted the handshake with a smile. His hands were strong and firm, easily covering up mine.

"Same here," he said, still holding my hands. "I hope we wouldn't be that much of a bother since we are kinda jumping in—"

"Oh no," I said. "You are welcome." When he finally released my hand, I bent to pick up my bag.

"Daphne over there has got herself a big catch," Madelyn whispered in my ears as I passed. "Did you see that fine ass on him?"

Using my free hand, I smacked her head. "Get your eyes off another woman's man."

I shook my head and walked away. I met with Lily and her husband, whose name was Tom. Tom had dirty brown hair, which was combed and brushed to the side. He was short, fit, and average-looking. I was a bit surprised because with how glamorous Lily was, one would think she was the wife of a Hollywood star. They were just so different. I wonder how exactly Daphne had thought they were a perfect match.

Love was like a lit candle. Sometimes it got blown off by the wind halfway, ending too soon. Sometimes, it got blown off by the couple themselves. Other times, it stayed till the candle burned out. Many people got together for all the wrong reasons, money, physical appearance, and not a beautiful personality.

Everyone liked the idea of a beautiful and rich partner. Three months into the relationship, once their eyes got used to the beauty, they started to see their partner's true nature. All the perfectness their brain made them believe turned out to be false. Then, of course, they seek to end things.

I froze when I wondered if it related to the relationship Ben and I had. I had fallen for him because of who he was. He was intelligent and kind and we had a lot of things in common. He was the kind of person you could read a book with, enjoying the comfortable silence while, getting lost in a beautiful fictional love. But what if Ben had fallen for me... because of my looks? Was there something about me that just didn't satisfy him?

I jumped, almost losing my balance when fingers snapped before me. "Earth to Amelia!" I blinked twice, holding my chest. "What were you thinking about?" Madelyn asked.

"Nothing," I said, breathing heavily. She looked like she was going to say something but decided against it. She gave me a small smile, squeezing my shoulders a little.

Soon, we had all our bags packed. When space ran out, the men helped Josh place some loads on the roof of the car. Lily, Tom, Daphne, and Anthony were going to travel in Lily's BMW, trailing us.

"OK, let's get this trip started!" Josh yelled. We cheered.

Chapter 5

The ride took us deep into the woods, where the only view was tall trees and grasses. Our car overheated twice, reminding me how old it was and how I needed to get a new car. We also got lost once. Josh had gotten confused and had taken a right turn instead of a left. Luckily, a kind stranger pointed us in the right direction. We got there after sunset when afterglow blessed the sky. A dark sheet soon spread across the sky as the glow got dimmer with each passing second.

The cabin looked old. Even Josh was surprised and thought we had arrived at the wrong place. He tried to call his father but couldn't reach him. "Just great," he said, putting his phone back in his pocket. "Well, this should be the place."

"Haven't you been here before?" Heather asked as we came out of the car.

"Well, that was when I was still little," he said. "We haven't visited this place for years. A few months ago, my cousins were here for a camping trip. They didn't stay long, though. The good news is we wouldn't meet with years of dust."

The cabin wasn't small, which was a good thing. I was worried that it would be cramped with the eight of us. It was night already, and the whole area was quiet and gave off an eerie feeling. The hairs at the back of my neck stood. I hugged myself, letting out a low whistle through my teeth while looking around the house.

"It's not so bad," Heather said. She was always one to think positively. "Josh, you said there were four rooms, right?" Josh nodded. "Well, you take one, and Lily and Tom take the other. Daphne and Anthony take one, and Amelia, Madelyn, and I will take the last room." In just a few seconds, she had already planned the sleeping arrangements.

Heather made it sound so easy, but I regretted coming already. With the eight of us, I was not too fond of the idea of waiting forever to use the bathroom or hurrying because someone wanted to use it after me.

"Yeah," Josh nodded. "It's already late, and I'm so tired. We could talk about other arrangements tomorrow. Let's just go sleep now." So we got our bags down and walked to the cabin.

The steps leading up to the front door moaned under our weight. I hurried to get to the porch, afraid that it might break. Madelyn laughed at me. "Scaredy cat," she said. I showed her my tongue and rolled my eyes.

Just as she was climbing up, Madelyn hurried too fast, slipped, and fell. Her palms saved her from hitting her head on the wall. "Are you Ok?" I asked her. Anthony, who had been behind her, helped her get back on her feet.

She looked at me. "I think that was a punishment for laughing at you."

"This is so cool," I heard Lily say. "It's like one of those haunted houses you see in movies. Josh, did someone die here? Are we expecting a ghost?" Everyone laughed at that.

"Don't be silly," Josh said, stepping forward, still chuckling. "There is no ghost, and there has been no death—not that I know of. It's not so bad on the inside, I promise." He placed the key into the lock, turning it open.

Josh was right. It wasn't bad on the inside. The chairs and tables were covered with some waterproof nylon to keep the dust away. I spotted some cobwebs coating the ceiling, but it was nothing a little cleaning couldn't fix. There were paintings on the wall, but none of them contained Josh or any member of his family. Most of them were landscapes. We had to turn on torchlights as there was no power.

"I will fix the power generator tomorrow," Josh said.

"Josh, who exactly did this cabin belong to?" I asked, my hands tracing the patterns on the vase that sat on a table beside the wall. I looked back at my fingers. They were dirty with dust. Since there was no water around to wash them, I just cleaned up at the back of my jeans.

"My grandfather," he said. "He was an artist. Those are a few of his works, and most of them are back at home."

"Cool," Someone muttered.

"There are two bedrooms downstairs and two upstairs," Josh said as we looked around. "The ones upstairs are bigger.

You guys should take it." He said to Anthony and Tom, who would be sharing the rooms with Lily and Daphne. "You girls can manage one, right?" He asked me. "Oh, will any of you want to share a room with me?" He wiggled his eyebrows jokingly at Heather, putting an arm over her shoulder.

She shot her tongue out, pushing him away. "You're staying alone, Josh. Madelyn, Amelia, and I will take one room." Although Josh and Heather were just friends, he often flirted with her. Sometimes I thought he had a crush on her.

He sighed. "It's going to be cold at night, and I could have offered the perfect body heat. But fine, your loss." He turned to the others. "I think we should all rest tonight and do cleaning tomorrow. You guys will find your rooms upstairs."

"Let's go, Tom," Lily said, grabbing her husband's hand. "If we get there first, we could get the best room."

"Not on my watch," Anthony said. Before we could say another word, he raced upstairs.

"Fuck," Lily cussed, running after him. Daphne and Tom followed behind, not seemingly interested in whichever room they ended up in.

With the aid of torchlight, Heather, Madelyn, and I found our way through the thick darkness. Our room was right beside the room Josh would be in. Madelyn stepped forward, pushing the door open. We followed quickly, curious to see the inside. The room was simple, but I liked the huge mirror laid against the wall by the wardrobe. It had beautiful patterns imprinted on it. There were two twin beds in there.

One was close to the window, while the other was close to the wardrobe.

"This isn't so bad," Heather said. "It's better than I imagined."

"Yeah," Madelyn agreed.

"I call bed by the window!" I shouted, running to the bed before anyone could claim it. "You guys can take the other bed," I said, turning back to see their shocked faces.

"Hey, not fair," Madelyn said with a pout. "Why do you get a bed all to yourself while Heather and I share the other?" She looked over at the other bed, then back at me.

"Yeah, I would like a bed all to myself too," Heather said but was already walking over to the other bed. "Madelyn, why don't you share with Amelia?"

I huffed. "Why? Because it's Heather's fault that I don't get a room to myself, and you're the one who made me come. That's all the explanation I'm giving you." I crossed my arms before my chest, ready for an argument.

"All right. All right," Madelyn muttered and walked to the other side of the room, which surprised me. She wasn't one to give up easily. "Urrgh! We need to clean this room before we can sleep here. I'm afraid a spider might crawl on me or worse, a cockroach." She pinched her nose, looking around the room. "What's that smell? I can't be the only one whose nose is working, right?"

I sniffed the air, and she was right. "Maybe some rotten food or worse, a dead rat?"

I climbed my bed to open the window. The air inside the room felt stuffy. I hadn't even been here for a full minute, and I was already sweating.

Heather sighed. "Madelyn, help me drag this off." Waterproof nylon was placed to protect the beds from dust. "Hold on to the other end." She instructed. Together they pulled it off. I did the same to my bed, coughing at the dust from the nylon.

"It's good they put the waterproof everywhere. My bones are weak, and my eyes tired," I told Madelyn. "Can't we just sleep and do cleaning tomorrow?"

She shook her head. "No, no, no. We can't sleep in this environment—Oh, look! Amelia, there's a broom beside your bed." I groaned out loud, kicking my foot out in frustration. I didn't just find a broom. I found two. There were also rags and window wash.

"Who kept the whole cleaning equipment in this room?"

We spent the next thirty minutes cleaning the room, and we found where the bad smell was coming from. Just under the bed where Madelyn and Heather would be sleeping was a rat skeleton. It had maggots all over it. From the looks of it, the rat must have died a long time ago.

"Fuck, I'm not touching that," Madelyn screamed, running away.

"I'm not touching it either," Heather said. They both turned to look at me.

"What?" I asked. I ended up carrying the rat out. I threw it through the window, using great force so it would go far away. After that, I had to close the window. "Can we just sleep?" Even Madelyn, who had suggested the cleaning, was tired.

"You sure you don't want to search around for any more dead rats?" Heather asked. "Or an alive one?"

"No, I don't think there's another one," Madelyn said, still spraying air freshener around the room. "That smell is from the dead one. And if there's any living creature here, we would only know if it crawled on us."

"That didn't make me feel better, Madelyn."

"It wasn't supposed to."

It didn't help that after cleaning, there was no water to take a bath. Josh had asked us to go to sleep. He will work on the water pump tomorrow morning. So, that's how our first night was spent in the cabin.

Chapter 6

I woke up at eight the next morning. I was used to waking up late, so my body wasn't okay with the sudden switch. This put me in a grumpy mood. The noise that woke me up came from outside. My right eye twitched in irritation as I held myself back from going out and taping everyone's mouth shut.

The door opened. "Good morning," Madelyn greeted me when she noticed I was awake. "Good, you're awake. I was wondering how much longer you could take all the noise." She had changed from the clothes she wore last night. She had on shorts and a polo, and she also had an apron tied around her neck. From the looks of it, she had taken her bath already, which meant Josh had been able to get the tap water running. I looked forward to a long bath.

"Good morning," I said. "What's with all the noise outside?" I rubbed my eyes as I sat up, brushing away my blonde locks from my face.

"The tap wasn't running, so Josh and Tom tried to fix the pumping machine to the well. That's where we got water to take our baths. Anthony is working on the generator. The girls are helping," she said.

"Oh." I watched her as she went through her bag. "How was your night?" I asked. "Sleep well?" I had a rough night initially. The heat and my sticky skin weren't a pleasant combination. Also, it didn't help that Madelyn had chosen this night to be a loud snorer. I wanted to go over to her bed and shut her mouth, but I was too tired.

"I wish," she said, rolling her eyes. "You're lucky you didn't share a bed with Heather. We should have just put her with Josh. She is a kicker." She rubbed her butt as she said that. Heather must have slept well then.

"What?" I asked, laughing. I knew what she was talking about, though. I shared a bed with Heather when we had a sleepover at Madelyn's family house. Let's just say the next morning, I woke up on the floor.

She sighed. "I was tempted to tie her legs together. At a time, she pushed me out of the bed. It took all in me not to carry and dump her outside in the woods." She shook her head. Then with a louder tone, she said, "This night, I'm sleeping with you. I'm not going through last night again."

"No problem," I said, kicking my legs out of bed and standing up. "I better go see what's happening outside. I don't want to be the only one who isn't helping."

"Oh, if you want to help, then you can help me in the kitchen. I'm trying to cook up some spaghetti and meatballs for breakfast."

I groaned. "No cereal?" I was used to taking light breakfasts, and cereal fit perfectly in that category, though spaghetti and meatballs sounded nice too. "I was looking forward to cereals."

She gave me a look as she walked to the door. "Cereal?" She laughed. "You should be lucky we're not eating just bread. We've got nothing here. We plan to go into town later and get some foodstuff," she said, walking out and closing the door behind her.

When I stepped out, I noticed a big difference in the cabin. It appeared they had done some cleaning while I was asleep. The cobwebs were nowhere to be seen on the ceiling, and the dust didn't coat the vases anymore. The waterproof had been removed and the chairs and tables put in the proper place.

I didn't know anything about cooking, so I helped with the little chores as Madelyn did all the work with the little ingredients we could gather. It smelled delicious. Madelyn was a good cook. Her family owned a big restaurant back in town. When we went on summer holidays, she would go help there, and we were always around to eat her delicious dishes.

While the food was cooking, I decided to take out the trash. "I'll be back. Let me drop this," I said to Madelyn. The morning was beautiful, and the birds were singing. The gentle breeze flowed along, creating a rustling sound as it brushed through the leaves of the trees. Combined with the chatter coming from the others, the cabin seemed to have come alive overnight.

"Good morning," I greeted as I hurried past Heather and Daphne, who were sitting on swinging armchairs by the front porch. They held a glass of orange juice as they chatted.

"Good morning," They both said. I hurried away. Ants had gathered in the trash, and I was trying to dump the trash before they crawled up my arms.

Lily was standing beside Anthony by the generator. The two were on a topic of their own. Anthony said something that made Lily laugh out loud. I dumped the trash in an empty trash bin in the backyard and headed back to the cabin, holding my arms far out. Some wet sticky juice from the trash had found its way to my hands, and it smelled terrible.

"Good morning, Amelia," Anthony greeted me as he saw me walking by. Lily wasn't by his side anymore.

"Oh morning, I didn't see you there," I said with a nervous laugh. That was a lie. I did see him, but I wasn't good at interacting with new people. I looked down at the generator, which was running. "You got it to work?"

"Yeah, it proved hard at first," he said. "Wasn't much of a big deal, though." He stretched his arm out a little, flexing his muscles. I held my eyes straight to his face. Since he was shirtless, I didn't want to look down and make him think I was checking him out.

"Well, that's good work. Thanks," I said laughing, hoping it didn't come out forced. "I better go. I need to go wash my hands." He nodded, and I walked back inside.

Heather and Daphne later drove to the nearest convenience store to buy food and supplies. We had seen the store on our way to the cabin. The guys went out to explore the woods, leaving us girls at home.

Lily was talking about her honeymoon again and how lavishly she had spent her money on things. "Tom is always complaining," she said. "But we only live this life once. I can't take my money with me when I die. I've got to enjoy it while I'm still alive."

Madelyn chuckled. "True. So, Daphne introduced you two to meet?"

"Yeah. Daphne is a true friend. I had just gone through a bad breakup. My ex, the bastard, tried to dupe me of five million dollars." I choked on my saliva, sitting up straight.

"Sorry," I said. "Did you just say five million dollars?" She nodded. I looked to Madelyn, who was also shocked.

"Anyways, Tom is different, you know. He is the first man I've met who isn't after my money. He cares for me. A year after we began dating, he asked me to marry him, and I said yes." She giggled. "Tom can be very jealous. Every time he sees me talking to a man, he thinks I'm planning on leaving him." She shrugged. "He just cares about me."

"Well," Madelyn said. "Don't we all love a jealous— Woah! Your necklace. It's beautiful."

Lily looked from the ornament around her neck back to Madelyn. "Thank you. Do you want it?" She asked.

"Oh no, I couldn't ask that from you." Madelyn refused, shaking her head.

Lily laughed, reaching to unhook the necklace. "If you like it, you can have it." And even though Madelyn kept on refusing, she collected the necklace when Lily handed it over to her. "And don't worry, Tom didn't buy that for me," Lily said.

"Ok, I'd like to have friends like you around me all the time." Madelyn giggled, hurrying to wear the necklace. "Amelia never spends her money on me."

Chapter 7

"We're back!" Heather announced, kicking the door open with her right leg. She strolled in, Daphne right behind her. They were holding two big bags in both their arms.

"Geez," Lily said, laughing at Daphne, who almost lost her steps due to the load she was carrying. "What did you two get?"

"Anything we could get our hands on, fresh meat, noodles, vodka, and cereals," Heather said, glancing at me. I gave a grateful smile. "Chips, tissues, you name it!" Heather hurried to the kitchen. A loud thump sounded as she dropped the items on the floor. "There is still some stuff in the car," she said from the kitchen. "You guys go bring them in."

The girls had bought many things. There were foreign sweets and chocolates, as Heather had a sweet tooth. My eyes widened when I saw a pack of condoms. I showed it to Madelyn. "Why did they buy this?"

She chuckled. "It looks like some people plan to get laid. I don't want to hear any moans while I'm trying to sleep. I wouldn't hesitate to go pound my fist on their doors if that happened."

Daphne blushed when she saw the condoms in my hand. "Don't mind Heather. She bought that just to mess with me."

Since Madelyn was too tired to cook, we settled down with potato chips and the sour chocolate the girls bought. "Why did you even waste money on this?" Madelyn asked, spitting the sour chocolate back in the pack. She threw the pack into the trash, but she missed and had to get up to put it properly.

"Hey, don't waste food," Heather reprimanded. She took a big chomp from the chocolate. "By the way, I like it." She grinned, showing us her chocolate-stained teeth.

"Ewww, how can you even say that?" Lily asked, her face scrunched up in disgust. "This tastes like what I suspect horse poop tasted like." She turned to Daphne, who hadn't even opened the pack she held.

"Don't look at me," Daphne said, raising her hand. "Once I saw the strange language on the pack, I told her it was a bad idea, but she didn't listen to me."

Heather scoffed. "I like to try out new things." She turned to me, smiling when she saw the chocolate pack in my hands was empty. "See, someone knows good taste. Amelia is done with hers."

"No," Madelyn said, returning to her seat. "She was the first to throw hers in the trash can. Nobody likes whatever poison that was." I gave a nervous laugh, avoiding Heather's eyes.

"Fine, I'll finish it myself," Heather muttered.

"You do that," Madelyn told her. "I'm going to cook up some noodles for lunch. I can't take this hunger no more. Heather, did you get the fresh carrots I asked you to buy?"

"Oh, I knew I forgot something. Sorry, Mads."

"It's all right," Madelyn said, walking to the kitchen.

The guys were back just when Madelyn was dishing the meal out.

"How was the trip?" Lily asked. "Did you find anything exciting or see any snakes? Chipmunks? or even more cool, a bear? Did you see any bears out there?"

"Eh..." Josh wasn't sure how to answer her question.

"Oh, trust me, Lily," I said. "There are no bears out there. If there were, Josh wouldn't have brought us here. He's terrified of bears."

Josh shot me a look. "Who wouldn't be? They are dangerous animals." He came to his defense quickly. "Everybody should be terrified of bears."

"I'm not," Lily told him. "I think they are cute and cuddly creatures." I didn't know if Lily had mistaken them for Winnie the Pooh, in red shirts holding jars of honey.

Anthony laughed, pinching her cheeks as he walked past. "If only you knew, darling. I've had an encounter with a bear once." This caught everyone's attention.

"Really?" Lily asked.

"Yeah, once, but nothing happened. My father, my brothers, and I had gone on a hunting trip. We saw a beat with her two cubs."

Lily turned to her husband, who had walked to her side. "Maybe after this, we could go visit the zoo? I've seen them on television, but never up close."

"You sure?" Tom stated. "I thought you wanted to travel the world."

She giggled. "I will if I can. This life is short. I have to enjoy it while I can."

Tom frowned. "Don't speak like that. One would think you're about to die anytime soon." She rolled her eyes and pushed his chest playfully. I resisted the urge to stick out my tongue at their cuteness. Instead, I chomped down harder on my chips.

"Are you guys going to keep talking, or are you ready to eat!" Madelyn shouted from the kitchen. "I'm so hungry I could eat all this myself. Don't test me."

Chapter 8

Dear Diary,
   It's been two days since we came here, and things are going smoothly. I've made friends with Daphne, who is such a sweetheart. Lily could be a little too much sometimes. But so far, we get along.

"OK, let's play a game of truth and dare," Heather suggested as we all sat around a campfire, a bottle of beer in everyone's hands except me. I held a bottle of coke, as my taste buds were not willing to take alcohol. Heather had a blanket wrapped around her up to her chin because of the chilly air. I didn't bring a sweater, so I settled for one of Josh's shirts.

"What do we look like, a bunch of high schoolers?" Madelyn asked, then took a swing from her beer. Madelyn was wearing just skimpy singlets and some shorts, proving that the cold wasn't affecting her. Sometimes, I thought of her as an alien.

"Come on," Josh said. "It will be fun. Who said the game was made for high schoolers only? You make it seem like we're old. Besides, there seems to be nothing else to do." Honestly, staring up at the beautiful sky while the evening breeze fanned my face was all I needed.

I kept quiet as I watched them arguing, but something else caught my attention. It was Lily and Anthony who were lost in a conversation of their own. They looked really close to each other. While I shouldn't have read anything into it, it just raised my eyebrows how they could be so comfortable with each other while their partners were around. I looked to Daphne, who didn't seem to be bothered by this. She was busy trying to convince Madelyn to play the game. I turned to Tom, who sat beside Josh. His eyes were on them, a stern look on his face, his lips set to a thin line. I remembered when Lily told us how jealous Tom could get. Honestly, I wouldn't blame him.

"Amelia," Heather called my attention. "What do you think?" She asked.

I blinked, I tried to recall the subject at hand, but I was lost. "Think about what?"

Madelyn sighed, not bothering to answer my question. She turned back to Heather. "Fine," she said. Heather gave a victory whoop.

"Let's play a game, but not truth or dare. How about never have I ever? It's more fun." Madelyn said. Heather opened her mouth to speak, but closed it back, then nodded her head instead. "Great." She turned to me. "Who's in?" Everyone said they would play, except me.

"I will sit this one out," I told Heather. During games like this, I preferred watching it instead of getting involved.

Sooner or later, they would get drunk. Lots of secrets would spill, better theirs than mine.

"Ok," Madelyn said, standing up. "I'll go get the drinks. I think Heather and Daphne bought a bottle of vodka the other day."

Soon, she was back with the vodka and seven shot cups. "Since we all know how the game works, no need to explain the rules." We all nodded. "I'll go first. Never have I ever kissed someone of the same sex." I giggled when I heard that. This would be fun.

We all looked around till Josh gave a sigh and reached forward for the vodka, pouring himself a shot. "One time, it was in high school, don't ask questions," he said quickly before downing his drink, squeezing his face at the spicy taste of the drink. For a moment, it looked like he was going to spit it out, but then it swallowed.

I laughed at the look on his face. "Don't tell us not to ask questions. I'm curious," I said, leaning forward. Josh and I attended the same high school along with Heather. So, saying that he kissed a boy, I would like to know who it was.

He glanced at me before looking away. "You will not like my answer, so don't ask." Now I was double interested. Everybody knew that telling someone not to ask was an invitation to be questioned.

"Tell us!" Heather urged, nudging his shoulders gently.

"Fine." He finally caved. "It was your brother," he said to me. "Alex."

It took my brain a while to understand what he had just said. "You're kidding, right?" I asked, but the look on his face was serious. "You kissed my brother? When? How? Where?"

"You see, this is why I didn't want to speak. One question will always lead to another. It was during a Halloween party. It was dark, Ok? He dressed like a witch. I thought he was Amanda Sternberg from twelfth grade. It turned out he wasn't. I only found out after we had kissed for about a second, and he pushed me away."

"Wait, was this the Halloween party that girl...what's her name again...Freya! Was it during the party she threw? Is this why you two were acting weird around each other for weeks?" I asked.

He nodded. I doubled over in laughter. I couldn't wait to go back home for Thanksgiving, and I would use this to tease the hell out of my brother. If I was lucky and he was still embarrassed about the incident, I could use it to demand a few favors from him. I smiled mischievously.

Josh eyed the look on my face suspiciously, but I ignored him. "Well, I've said mine. Who's next?" He asked, wiping his lips.

"That will be me," Heather said while still trying to control herself from laughing at Josh. She cleared her throat, brushing her hair back. She tied her hair back in a bun before she continued. "Ok, let's see...Oh, I have a good one. Never have I ever had a threesome." She looked around to see who would reach out.

No one reached forward for a while, and then Lily giggled, leaning forward to grab the vodka. "Fine, one time last year," she said.

"What?" I heard Tom ask before she could even bring the cup to her lips. The group became silent as we stared at the couple. I mean, I knew the game demanded that one be honest. But if I were to be playing a game like this with my partner and a question like this was asked, I would rather lie than admit to it. Better to protect my relationship than to adhere to the rules of some stupid game.

"It's not a big deal, Tom." She shrugged. It was like she didn't realize the effect of what she said. "It isn't like we were together at that time. I met you a few months after that. This was sometime after I broke up with my ex." I remembered that her ex had been the one who tried to dupe her of millions.

Tom didn't say anything for a while, and I prayed he would just let the matter die down than add fuel to the fire. "Do I know these people?" Now, that wasn't a wise question. If she said no, he would be angry. If she said yes, he would be even angrier.

"No," she said, shaking her head. "I don't even know who they are." I wondered if that additional information was supposed to lighten the issue. "Just some dudes I met one night at a club." I slowly turned to look at Tom. He looked pissed, which was an understatement to the unadulterated anger that showed in his eyes.

No one spoke a word as we waited for someone to try and clear the air. Heather came to the rescue. "Maybe we should stop the game now," she suggested. "It's getting kinda cold—"

"Oh no," Tom said, surprisingly calm. "It's my turn, and I'll go next." We all glanced at each other nervously. I could see Anthony from the corner of my eyes moving a little away from Lily. "Never have I ever cheated on my partner." Tom dropped.

I couldn't believe he just said that. I heard Lily gasp. "Fuck you, Tom!" Lily shouted, standing up. "What the hell is that supposed to mean?" Her palms were tight in a fist, her chest heaving as she breathed angrily.

"You tell me," he retorted just as angrily. "I'm not the one that goes about sleeping with random men," He spat.

"OK, guys, please calm down," Anthony said.

"You stay out of this!" Tom shot at him.

"You know," Lily spoke. "Maybe I did live a promiscuous life before we got married, but I've never cheated on you. I'm going to sleep." She stormed away. She got to the cabin, slamming the door so hard, I heard the windows rattle in their frames.

I stared down at my coke. The tension in the air held my muscles tight, and I didn't know what to say. An awkward silence reigned. "I'm sorry about that," I heard Tom say. "I'll go talk to her." He stood up and began walking to the cabin.

"Well, that took a surprising twist," Anthony said once Tom was gone. "He should have calmed down. What he said to her was just hurtful, and it isn't like she knew him when it happened."

"Right," Josh said. "But then Lily wasn't exactly wise with her words. Still, you shouldn't be angry at the things your partner did when they didn't even know you existed at that time."

"He's acting like he is a virgin," Madelyn said. All this while, Daphne kept quiet. She was staring at the cabin, at the upstairs window to Tom and Lily's room.

"I feel bad. I was the one who suggested we played the game," Heather said in a low voice.

"Don't. From the look of things, they had the fight coming up sooner or later," Madelyn told her. "Well, I'm retiring to bed. See you folks tomorrow."

"You're going already?" I asked.

"Well, the mood of the night has been ruined already. Maybe we could continue another day, but now, I'm going to sleep." Madelyn said.

I was tired myself, and so were the others, so we all cleared out and headed inside.

Even as we slept that night, the voices of Tom and Lily were heard. It seemed instead of reconciling, they had continued with the fight. I glanced at Madelyn, who lay on the bed beside me. She was fast asleep, snoring lightly. She was always a heavy sleeper. I stayed up for a long time until the noise faded. Probably they got tired of shouting. Finally, I closed my eyes to sleep.

Chapter 9

Dear Diary,
It's been six days here on the camping trip and remember when I said I was having fun? Yeah, not anymore. The issue with Tom and Lily hasn't died down, and anytime both of them are in the room, the tension there becomes unbearable. I do hope they solve their issue fast, and it isn't helping that Lily seems to have taken a liking to Anthony, ignoring the fact that she's married or he has a girlfriend. I don't know. I must be reading into it too much.

Well, on the bright side, I haven't thought of Ben or our broken relationship for a few days now, so that's one good thing, at least.

"OK, I just have to bring this up," I said out loud. "I don't feel comfortable here anymore."

Heather looked at me. "Same." We were the only ones in the house, except for Tom, who was upstairs in his room. The others had gone to a river nearby to swim. "Things are not going as we had planned." She let out a huge sigh, chewing one of the chocolates she bought the other day. She wasn't kidding when she said she was going to finish it herself. "I can't wait for us to go home."

I also would like to go back home. Anthony and Daphne were cool, and I had no problem with them, but Tom and Lily brought a whole different plate. Individually, they were cool. Together? Disaster. I didn't know what they saw in the other that made them think they were perfect for each other. It was just the early months of their marriage, and they already fought this much. I couldn't help but wonder what would happen in years to come. This brought Ben to my head. Is it possible that our relationship could have gone this way? If he hadn't spoken up when he did, how long could he last before he exploded? The break-up was probably the best option.

"Were they always like this?" I asked. "Tom and Lily, I mean, do they fight all the time?" It had been four days now, and there was still cold blood between them.

"Not really. Although Lily can be a big flirt, I think they are mostly just innocent. Tom can be very jealous, and he over-thinks. He's always reminding her that what most men want from her is her money. I think he uses this as a way to somehow...keep her away from other men?" She shrugged. "I dunno."

"That's not a very nice thing for him to say to his wife and the way he speaks to her..." I paused, looking around before I continued, "I wouldn't be surprised if that's why she flirts with other men. Lily seems close to Anthony, though, and I can't be the only one who sees how they interact. Sometimes I wonder, are they just friends flirting? Or wannabe lovers?"

Heather shrugged. "I can't say—" She stopped when we heard a door upstairs being pushed open. It must be Tom. He had complained of headaches earlier and had been in bed since morning. We waited, our eyes glued to the stairs to see who would show up, although we already knew who we were expecting to see. But I was surprised to see Daphne show up, and she also looked shocked to see us as she let out a small scream, almost making me scream myself.

"Sorry, I wasn't expecting to see anybody here." She held to her chest, breathing heavily. "I thought you guys followed them to the...river? That's where they went, right?" I also thought Daphne had followed them to the river. I had seen her go out the doors with them.

"We decided to stay back," Heather told her. "Were you around the whole time?"

"Not really. I came back hours ago. I went back to the convenience store to get Tom medicine for his headache." She walked over and sat on the old sofa, just beside me. "So, what are you girls talking about?" She wiggled her eyebrows.

I bit my lips nervously, wondering if she had been eavesdropping on us. She was surprised when she saw us, so she probably just walked in. "Nothing much," I replied. "How's Tom feeling?" I decided to ask.

"Oh, he's fine," she said.

I smiled. Nobody had thought of checking on Tom to see how he was faring. Lily seemed to have moved on from the incident, but Tom still looked hurt. It was nice for Daphne to have checked on him. "You two must be good friends," I pointed out.

She nodded her head. "Yeah, Tom and I go way back, even before I met Anthony or he met Lily...well, I introduced him to Lily. So, of course, we ought to have met before that." She gave a little laugh. "I know they aren't on best terms with each other at the moment, but they are a sweet couple. When I first met Lily, I just knew they were going to be perfect together." That's something I would disagree with. Nearly a week with them, and I don't see the 'perfect couple.' "Though Lily can be too much sometimes, she's very nice. They will be fine."

"Is he still angry about what Lily said during the game?" I asked.

"Not really. That's one of the reasons I've been up in his room, explaining to him that he was wrong to have reacted that way. I've spoken to him and told him to apologize to Lily once she gets back," she informed us. "I trust him to do the right thing."

"Good," Heather said. "I know Lily is forgiving. He apologizes, and everything goes back to the way it was." She took a big bite from the bar of chocolate.

"How do you even enjoy that thing?" I asked. "You're putting yourself through pain. Just throw it away. It's ok sometimes for food to waste if it's trash."

"Don't speak ill words against my chocolate, Amelia. You guys just have problems with your taste buds." She defended, starting to chew aggressively.

***

Hours later, we heard chattering from outside. The others had returned. "You guys will not believe what I found at the river?" Josh said as they walked into the cabin, Madelyn just behind him. Both their hairs were wet.

"Let me guess, a bag of bones?" I gave a mock look of interest. "Or even more cool, did you see a bear?"

Josh shot out his tongue in a childish. "Ha-ha, very funny, Amelia." He rolled his eyes.

Heather giggled. "Don't mind her, Josh. Tell us what you found," she told him, leaning forward in interest.

"A knife," he said. Taking a seat beside her, he brought down his bag, a small bag he always carried around his shoulders. It didn't contain many things, just his camera, spare keys, and a gold tooth that had belonged to his great-grandfather. I didn't even want to ask why he carried that.

I frowned, confused. "A knife? That's the interesting stuff you found?" I was expecting some more exciting tale like fresh bones that washed up the river shore or some ancient book of spells. I've always found them fascinating, even though I didn't believe in magic.

"Not just any knife," Madelyn said, taking a seat beside me. "Show them, Josh." If Madelyn wasn't bored, it meant he must have found something unusual.

He nodded. Opening his bag, he brought out a small knife. It was simple looking and plain, nothing fancy about it, but I liked the way it was curved. It was also painted gold. "It's made entirely out of gold."

"Shut up," I sat up quickly. "Real gold? That's real gold?"

He nodded excitedly. "Now you're interested. I don't know if the blade is gold, but this handle looks gold to me... If it is real gold, do you know how expensive this will be? I could get good cash from this, get a first-class trip to the Bahamas." Just then, Lily and Anthony entered, both of them laughing. Heather and I shared a look when we saw this. I looked at Daphne, but she didn't seem to care much. She was more interested in the knife Josh was holding.

"How much do you think it's worth?" Daphne asked.

"I don't know," Josh shrugged. "But it must be pretty expensive. Do you want to feel?" He asked. She nodded quickly.

"Are you going to sell it?" Madelyn asked. "You could get some cool cash off that."

"Yeah, I know, right." he nodded. "I'm not sure yet."

"Hey," Anthony said to Daphne as he walked over to her. Leaning down to lay a chaste kiss on her lips. "I hope you didn't miss me too much?" He teased, pulling her hair gently.

She scoffed. "You wish." Pushing him away.

"Has Tom been in bed all day?" Lily asked, looking toward the stairs. "I haven't seen him since I left the room this morning. Did he come downstairs?"

"No," Heather answered. Lily sighed and walked toward the kitchen. Heather stood up also. "I will go talk to her."

"How long do you think they are going to remain like this?" Madelyn asked. "Can't they just kiss and make up? Reunion sex is the best. It's crazy, wild, and beautiful."

"Oh, Mads," I muttered, palming my head.

"Trust me," she said, her eyes twinkling. "I am speaking from experience."

The others laughed. "I'm sure you are," I said.

Chapter 10

The next morning I was surprised to see Tom and Lily together. They had bright smiles on their faces, and no sign of anger or malice in their tone as they spoke to each other. Tom had kept to his words, as Daphne told us yesterday. I was glad they had solved their issue. Today we planned to hike to a nearby creek the guys had discovered coming back from the river. With everyone now in a jovial mood, we might have fun again.

"Amelia, where are you?" I heard Madelyn shout my name from outside. "We need to go now." I sighed. Something about the way she called me felt like Déjà vu. Madelyn was always the first to wake up in the two of us. Whenever we planned to go out, I was used to the whole 'Amelia, where are you?' question.

I closed the windows, locking them. "I'm coming!" I threw a torchlight into my bag, zipping it, and I ran out of the room. I blushed, somewhat embarrassed when I saw I was the last to finish packing. Everyone was outside already. We weren't carrying much load since we would be back the following day, just sleeping tent, food, mosquito repellent, and of course, beers. "Ok, let's go!" I cheered.

Josh led the group with Heather and Madelyn. Lily and Tom were behind. Then there were Daphne and Anthony while I slagged off behind lazily. The woods were tranquil. The only sound was the chirps from the birds above and the rustling of the leaves from the trees around. The clouds above and the dense trees protected us from the scorching sun.

I couldn't help but think about some undead soldier from the thirteenth century running toward me while waving an ax around. I blamed the book I read last night. It told the story of a young soldier who had been accused of sleeping with his general's wife. He had been ripped of his position, disgraced publicly, and hanged. Just when everyone thought that was the end of it, he returned from the dead to seek revenge on the people whose accusation had led to his death. However, the undead soldier only haunted at night. Now, the sun still blessed Earth with its light.

I stopped to catch my breath. I was thirsty, hot, and in pain. "Josh, how far is this creek?" I asked in a raised voice, hurrying up to meet him. When I finally caught up with him, my feet were on fire.

"Not too far from the river," he said. "If your bag is too heavy, I could help you with it."

"Never mind. I barely carried anything since it's just one night." I was more concerned about my feet than my bag. I was relieved when Josh said the creek wasn't so far but then realized something else. "And how far is the river?"

His eyes widened. He looked at me but turned away quickly as if avoiding my eyes. "Eh... it's a little far. Don't worry. We'll get there soon."

"Yay!" I said dryly. "If we haven't gotten there in minutes to come, I don't care how tired you are, and you're carrying me. The boots I have on aren't for hiking. I haven't trimmed my toenails for a while. They are pushed hard against the boots with each step I take, and it's getting very painful."

Lily began to tell a story about an experience she had during her honeymoon. Before, I didn't realize why Lily talked so much about her honeymoon, but then I got to understand that she told it many times only because it meant so much to her. "And I told Tom that was the last puzzle to finally escape the room, he was to pull the lever up, but he didn't believe me. Right, Tom?" Tom nodded. "He thought it was a clue to another riddle. After trying hard, I couldn't pull it." She giggled, looking down at her small arms. "I had to drag Tom by his ears before he finally did it." She grabbed hold of Tom's hand. "This is Tom's strength. He's left-handed, you know. Which is good for him because Tom's right hand is still weak because of the accident."

"Accident?" I asked curiously, looking over at Tom's hand. "You guys got involved in an accident?"

"Not me, just Tom. It's nothing big. Just before our wedding, Tom got in an accident. That's why he was wearing a cast on his right hand. You saw it, right? I showed you the wedding photos." I nodded. The first day I met Lily, she showed us pictures from her honeymoon and wedding.

"How's your arm?" Josh asked Tom.

"It's healing," Tom replied.

Minutes later after my grumbling and complaining in Josh's ear, we finally arrived at the creek. It was beautiful. The water was clear turquoise blue, dancing on its path. It ran through the forest, hopping over hard rocks. The sun, which created beautiful glitters on the surface, made them shiny. With the tall trees and waving leaves, all this gave off a heavenly vibe.

"Woah, Josh," Lily said. "I've never been to a place like this before. This is lovely."

"I know right," Josh said with a proud smile. "There's a clear path nearby, and we can settle over there for the night." He led us to the place he talked about, just a stone's throw away.

The first thing I did was remove my boots and sit on a huge rock beside a big tree. The umbrella above protected me from the sun. I began to massage my sore toes. When I got back to the cabin, the first thing I would do was clip off my toenails. The others started to set up the camping tent.

Madelyn looked over at me. "Amelia, you can't just sit there," she complained. "Aren't you coming to help?"

I gave her a lazy smile, leaning back to rest my head. "Leave me alone Madelyn. My feet hurt." She shot me a look but didn't complain anymore. I didn't know how much time passed. When Madelyn woke me from the little nap I was taking, they were done with everything. I gave a loud yawn, rubbing my eyes as I smiled cheekily at Madelyn. "Wow, you guys finished up fast."

"Yeah, but we would have finished even faster with a little extra hand from you, but someone was lazy." I ignored her sass. Grabbing onto the hand she held out, I stood up. "We are going to go get a group photo over by the river," she informed me. "Finally, Josh can put his camera to use. I don't think he's taken even one photo with it ever since he bought it."

"I heard that!" Josh shouted from where he stood with Anthony.

"You were supposed to!" She shouted back.

We all went to wash our faces first, then changed into the best outfits we had come with. We found the perfect spot where our background was tall trees, and the creek crashed against the huge rocks. "Ok!" Josh shouted, running back. "I've set the timer. Everybody smile."

The flash went off.

The photo came out great. Lily, Daphne, Heather, and I had bright smiles on our faces. Josh and Madelyn seemed like they were ready to get into another argument. Anthony had on a silly face, his hands spread out in the air while Tom, well, Tom looked like how Tom always looked on a typical day.

"You should smile more," Lily told her husband.

Chapter 11

"And then she was never seen again," Josh concluded the scary story he had been telling us. "Though," he continued. "At midnight, they said if you go by the creek, you will hear the voice of the weeping widow." He glanced around to see the effects of his words on us. We all sat around the fire, staring wide-eyed at him, but Anthony had a wide smile on his face. The story hadn't gotten to him one bit. "She pulls people to the creek with her cries and tries to drown them." I couldn't remember the movie exactly, but I was sure I'd watched a horror movie that had the same plotline as Josh's story.

"Wait, what about her son, Edward?" Heather asked, hugging her knees close to her chest. "What happened to him?" She questioned, though from the look in her eyes, I didn't think she wanted to know what happened to Edward. Heather got scared easily. Whenever we had movie nights, and the genre was horror, she would give some excuse and run away. On the days she couldn't come up with one, she missed half the movie as she stared more at the floor than the screen.

"His body was found weeks later floating around in the river, though he did say he would return to have his revenge." I rolled my eyes. This was like the beginning of some horror movie. It always started with some group of teenagers or young adults going into the woods to camp, and then a witch came and killed every one of them. Though the movie producers made it seem like the lead character would survive, the witch you thought was gone would always come back.

I shot Josh a look. "And you didn't just make this all up?"

He let out a heavy sigh. "You don't believe me?" He questioned. "Fine. Could I take you guys to the cabin? The guys and I passed it when we had gone exploring the other day, right?" He turned to Anthony, who nodded.

"Though, the cabin looked normal to me, just abandoned," Anthony said with a shrug.

"Hey, I have an idea," Madelyn spoke up. "How about we go visit this 'haunted' house, just for fun." I looked at Madelyn like she was crazy. She noticed this and gave a toothy grin. "Come on, Amelia, it will be fun."

"No!" Heather was quick to say. "Are you crazy? We need to stay away from stuff like that. This is madness. When you see danger, you run away from it, not head toward it because you think it will be fun."

Madelyn rolled her eyes. "Come on, Heather. Don't you think some widow and her son are going to come after us? I bet you this story was just made up to scare people away, a bunch of bullshit." She turned to Josh. "Right, Josh?" He shrugged.

"I do like the idea," I said. Heather snapped her head to me, and she had on the look I had just given Madelyn seconds ago. Now I was the crazy one. "I mean, it's going to be fun, we'd come here to have fun, so we might as well do this." I turned to Josh. "Is the house far away from here?"

"Not at all," he said. "You guys really want to do this?" He looked surprised.

"No." Heather stood up. "I am too young to die. I have plans, have a dream, and want to get married and have kids before I die. You guys can go. I'll stay here and wait."

"You sure you want to stay here," Anthony said. "Alone?" He added. "You never know what might be in the woods." Heather shot him a look, and you could see his words got to her. He laughed. "Don't mind me."

"Urrgh!" She groaned, stumping her feet angrily. "Fine, I'll come. But if something happens to me and I die? I swear, my spirit will not rest. I'll haunt you all till you die," she threatened.

We all laughed it off. Heather could be dramatic whenever she was scared or worried. "It will be fine, Heather," I said to her.

***

We put off our campfire, each carrying a torchlight. We set off, Josh leading us again.

"This is a bad idea," Heather kept saying. Whenever she heard a little noise, she would scream and grab hard at the person next to her, which was me. My arm started to hurt from how hard she squeezed. Sometimes she would hold it hard for so long, and I would feel my hand going numb.

"Calm your pants down," Lily said. "Anyways, I don't believe in ghosts. This kind of stuff doesn't scare me." This surprised me because if anyone, I would think Lily would be scared the most.

"We're almost there, guys," Josh announced after we had been walking for a while. "There," he said. "I can see it now." He hurried in his steps, and we followed behind.

Compared to this cabin, Josh's was heaven. This cabin looked like it was cut out from a Halloween magazine and placed right here in the woods. "Woah," Madelyn was the first to speak. "Ok, I agree with Heather. We should go back."

"Oh, now you agree with me." Heather turned to Josh. "You don't plan for us to go in, right? Please, Josh, just... let's go back."

"Come on, Heather," Anthony said. "We're here, right? We might as well go in." He turned to Madelyn. "You're the one who suggested it in the first place. You can't back out. You owe this to Heather."

Madelyn scoffed. "Yeah, but I wasn't expecting this. Just look at this place. It's obviously haunted."

"Well, I don't believe in spirits or anything of the sort. I'm going in." Anthony said.

"I'll come with you!" Lily jumped eagerly, leaving her husband to walk over to Anthony's side. "I'm scared, but there's a first time for everything." Anthony nodded.

Everyone was thrown into an argument. In the end, Josh decided to stay back with Heather and Daphne, who both refused to come. The rest of us went in.

The interior was tidy. There were two single sofas facing a television from the nineties, the ones that I was sure would only show you black and white pics. There weren't any bones, ancient pots for rituals, spell books, weird occultic drawings, or anything I had expected to see. It was smaller than Josh's cabin. "I thought this house was supposed to be cursed or something?" Madelyn questioned. "I was expecting more. This is disappointing."

"Maybe someone comes to clean the house..." I spotted two bottles of beer lying on the floor beside one of the chairs. "Beer? Do ghosts drink beers?" I laughed, walking over to the chair. I picked one of the bottles and showed the guys.

Anthony laughed. "Well, I guess this is just another stupid tale to scare people. Let's leave. Nothing is—" A clang suddenly came from somewhere in the house.

We all stopped in our steps. No one spoke for a while as we listened for the sound again. I thought one of us had knocked something down, but the sound came from upstairs, not in the living room.

"What was that?" Lily asked in a fierce whisper. "I heard something. Did you guys hear that?" Like a reply to her question, it sounded again, this time like someone was slowly opening a door with rusted frames.

"Ok, I think we should—" No one waited for Anthony to finish speaking. The moment we heard footsteps approaching, we all raced out of the house, screaming. When

Josh, Daphne, and Heather saw us running out, they followed, not waiting to find out the reason behind our screams.

I ran blindly, not caring to look at the path I was taking, just following Josh. We kept on running till we got to a safe distance, where we stopped to catch our breath. "What happened? What did you guys see in there?" Heather asked, looking back to see if something was after us.

"Yeah, tell us. Did you see a witch?" Josh asked curiously. "Dang! I wish I had followed you guys."

"No, we didn't—cramp!" Madelyn tried to speak but doubled over, gripping her lower tummy. "Cramp!" She moaned in pain. "Can we just go home? Like out of this woods?"

Josh laughed. "Is Madelyn scared of a ghost?"

"Shut up." She shot him a look. "There was no ghost in the house...Ok, there was something."

"What was it?" Heather asked.

"I'm sorry, Heather, I couldn't stay to find out what it was because I love my life. Listen, you guys can stay here asking questions, but I'm going home." Madelyn turned in a direction and began to walk away.

"You're going the wrong way."

Chapter 12

I opened my eyes to find myself back at the haunted cabin, except this time, I was alone. "Hello," I called, confused. My echoes were the reply that came back, almost making my bones jump out of my skin from fear.

A candle was lit in the middle of the room, stuck to the floor by its wax. I took slow steps. For some reason, I had to make sure I made no sound at all. Something told me I could awaken trouble. I bent, picking up the candle, but just as I was about to grab it, the front door of the cabin was pushed open by a heavy wind. The door locks fell to the floor with a loud clang. I jumped up in fright, using my hands to protect my eyes from the dust the wind brought with.

I opened my eyes when the air went dry. Now I was in darkness. The wind had put off the candle. I could feel a presence in the room with me. I tried to turn, but my legs were stuck to the ground. Someone or something was behind me. The hairs on my neck were standing. I shivered as a cold chill ran down my spine. My suspicion was confirmed when I felt a heavy breath behind my ears.

"Amelia," I heard my name called softly. It was almost a whisper. It was a female's voice. I didn't know this voice, but my mind told me who the speaker was. The widow? She gave a low laugh, and then she was gone. I struggled and saw I could move my feet again. The door was pushed open once more.

Just when I was about to turn to look behind me. "Get out!" A voice screamed. I didn't need to be told twice. As fast as my feet could carry me, I ran out of the cabin.

I woke up in the middle of the night to Madelyn's screaming. "What's wrong?" I jumped up, my heart pounding against its cage. "You scared me!" I reached out for my torchlight and turned it on.

"Sorry," Madelyn said, her voice heavy. "I had a bad dream." She cleared her throat, giving me a sheepish look.

I frowned, remembering I just had one of my own. Was the story of the widow true? "Do you want to talk about it?" I asked.

"Eh...It's nothing. Let's go back to sleep." Before I could say another word, she laid back down. "Goodnight," she said.

A smile crept up my face as I bit my lips, struggling not to laugh. "Madelyn?"

"Mmmh?" She mumbled, turning to face me. Madelyn frowned when she saw the look on my face, already expecting what was coming.

"Did you see the weeping widow in your sleep?" I asked in my best impression of a witch's voice.

"No!" She shouted before the last words could even leave my lips, which confirmed my suspicion. I burst out laughing at Madelyn's embarrassment.

I laid my head back, going to sleep. "Ok, but you can hold my hands if you're scared," I teased. "I will protect you from the evils of this world."

"Fuck you," I heard her mutter. I went back to sleep, and this time I didn't have a bad dream.

The following day we packed everything and were on our way back to Josh's cabin. "Let's have a barbecue tonight," Daphne suggested. "I haven't had meat for days now."

"Yeah, let's have a barbecue." Heather nodded. "And it's good we have Madelyn with us. You could use your family's special sauce. You brought it, right?" She turned to face Madelyn.

"Yeah," Madelyn answered. "How could I have forgotten? You texted me every three hours threatening my life if I didn't bring it." I was actually the one who sent the message to Madelyn using Heather's phone, but I kept quiet when it was brought up.

"When have I ever threatened your life? I'm innocent of this accusation being thrown my way." Heather said in the most dramatic voice she could summon.

Madelyn scoffed. "That's not true, and if my battery wasn't dead. I would bring up your texts as evidence."

"Amelia." Heather turned to me. "Do I tell lies?"

I raised my hands. "You two shouldn't involve me. I just want to go back home and sleep." We continued, enjoying listening to the silly argument going on between Madelyn and Heather.

"Wait!" Josh said suddenly, making us stop. "Is my eyes deceiving me or..." He didn't have to continue. I saw what he was talking about. Two men, probably in their late thirties, were heading our way, carrying two heavy bags. It seemed they were in a hurry to get somewhere.

We studied them carefully. The woods could be dangerous, and you never know who or what you might stumble across, a poisonous snake, a bear, or worse, some serial killer. After we met them and had a short conversation, we found out that they had gone camping just like us and were heading home. I wondered if they were a couple. We exchanged goodbyes and wished them well before we continued on our way.

"Am I the only one whose heart skipped a beat when we saw them?" Lily laughed. "We should do this camping again, sometime. I've never been exposed to such an experience before, and I would like to visit here again." If we were ever going to come back to these woods, I had no problem with Lily coming with us, but she had to leave her husband behind. After this trip, I couldn't hear another one of their fights.

"Don't worry. Even if those men were dangerous, I could easily take them down," Anthony said and flexed his muscles, winking at Lily.

Lily giggled. "Good, I can count on you to always protect Daphne. Which gym did you say you usually worked at again?" She asked. We had just arrived back at the cabin.

"Tony's," he said. "Heard of it?" I have heard of the gym. In fact, Madelyn was thinking of signing up there sometime last year. Not because she wanted to lose weight or anything, but because she was after a boy. When she found out later that he had a girlfriend, she gave up.

"No," Lily answered, looking down at her tummy. "Maybe one day you could take me there, I could sign up too. I think I'm adding some fat."

"You're just fine," Tom said.

"Of course you will say that," she said. "Maybe Tom could sign up too." She grabbed Anthony's arms, feeling him up. "Woah, someone's buff." I looked to see Tom's reaction. He didn't look too happy with this.

Josh had opened the doors to the cabin. I hurried inside to go to our room.

"What the fuck!" Madelyn shouted. I stopped in my steps, turning to look back at her. It was then I noticed the state of the cabin. I had rushed past quickly, and it escaped my eyes.

"What happened here?" I questioned, hurrying back to the living room. The cabin had been thrown askew. Someone had raided the cabin while we were out last night. It was in a worse state than when we first arrived.

"Fuck," Josh cussed. "Is it possible that those men we saw?" We all shared a look, and then realization set in. No wonder their bags were so big. They were filled with stuff they took from our cabin. "Fuck!" Josh cussed. "I knew there was something familiar about that vase that was peeking out from one of their bags. Look—" he pointed to a table by the wall, where the vases had been previously arranged. One vase lay broken on the floor while the others were missing.

"We could go after them?" Anthony suggested.

"No need," Josh said. "They would be long gone by now. We don't need most of the items they took anyway. We locked our doors before we left yesterday, right?"

"I locked ours," I said. Tom and Anthony said they had locked theirs too.

"Tom, aren't you happy I reminded you to lock the doors," Lily said to her husband. "If you hadn't, I'm pretty sure they would have gotten their hands on my pieces of jewelry...those bastards!"

"Well, thieves can break locks, right?" Heather reminded us. "We should still check if any of our things are missing." As soon as Lily heard that, she let out a little yelp, running up the stairs to check. We waited till she showed up minutes later, looking relieved.

"Our door is intact. They didn't get in."

Fortunately, they couldn't break any of our doors or didn't even try. They had broken in through the kitchen window. That's why the locks to the front door were still intact when we arrived. They took vases, plates, some artwork on the walls, and even one of the packs of beers.

"Shit! They took the extension cord of the generator." Josh came back from outside. "We won't have power tonight. I will go into town to get a new extension cord tomorrow."

"We won't have electricity tonight?"

"Nope."

"That's just great." Madelyn threw her backpack to the floor.

We started to clean the mess the thieves had made. It took hours before we finally made the place tidy again.

"I can't believe those men would do something like this," Heather said once we were through. "They looked so nice."

"Well, you should remember that the evils of men aren't written on their foreheads," Anthony said. "I've met the most scary-looking men that turned out to be angels and sweet-looking people that turned out to be psychos." He turned to Josh. "We should do something about the broken window. We don't want them raiding the house while we sleep." Josh nodded. The two men walked away, heading to the kitchen.

"Well, now that we're done. I'm going to sleep." I said.

"You sleep a lot," Lily said and then gave a loud yawn. "Ok, I'm also going to sleep."

Chapter 13

The sweet smell from the barbecue had my mouth watering. I walked toward the picnic area located at the back of the cabin. Madelyn was grilling steaks, sausages, and corns.

My mind went back to the conversation I had with Lily on our way back from the creek. I wasn't one to hold back on my thoughts, so when the two of us were alone, I brought to her attention the way she was openly flirting with Anthony.

She threw her head back, laughing. "It's nothing," she said. "It's just innocent flirting, Amelia. Don't worry about it. Daphne doesn't seem to mind, and she knows it means nothing." She shrugged, brushing her hair back.

It was true Daphne didn't mind. If someone were flirting with my boyfriend, I would call it out and demand it stopped immediately. But it wasn't just about whether Daphne cared or not. It isn't something that one should do to a friend. Maybe Daphne did care but was too nice or shy to speak out. But it wasn't my business after all.

"Yeah, you're right. But what about Tom, your husband." I said.

"Tom? Oh, he has no problem with it. He has said it himself."

I was surprised by her response. He had no problem with it? I wondered if we were talking about the same Tom.

"Really?" I asked. It didn't look like 'He has no problem with it,' though. I knew the look I saw on Tom's face whenever Lily and Anthony were together. It wasn't a happy one.

"Trust me. It's just innocent flirting. I love Tom. I'll never cheat on him, and Daphne is a good friend. I will never do that to her. Who would even try to pursue their friend's partner? That's just evil."

I nodded. "Ok. I just don't want to see you get hurt." I said. She hugged me.

"Madelyn," Josh called. "How long is it going to take you? I'm starving!" He shouted.

"Why don't you come closer and ask me that question, Josh," Madelyn said sweetly, but there was a threatening tone laced with it. "All you're doing is sitting and eating chips while I'm working my ass off here." Josh's brows furrowed. I could tell he regretted opening his mouth as Madelyn waved her hot tong before him. "Say that again, and it will be your meat on this grill."

Josh looked like he was going to speak again but decided against it. He moved away to take a seat beside Heather. Heather laughed at the look on Josh's face, and she pulled him closer. "Don't worry. I'll protect you from the mean lady," she teased.

He turned to her with a smirk. "You sure about that? Is this just an excuse to feel my muscles?" He winked at her. She pushed him away immediately.

"Madelyn, if you want to kill him, you're free."

Josh gasped dramatically, holding his chest. He feigned a look that suggested his feelings were hurt. "Women are nothing but heartbreakers," he said.

Minutes later, just when my stomach was tired of singing from hunger, I heard the words I'd been waiting for. "They are ready," Madelyn announced. "Josh, bring the plates."

"Why me?" He asked but got up to help.

"If you're hungry, you'll do as I said." Soon dinner was served and dished out.

As soon as Josh handed a plate to me, I dived in for a piece. "Fuck!" I shouted, dropped the sausage, and sucked my fingers. It was just removed from the grill and was still hot.

"Sorry," Josh said. "Did you hurt yourself?" He asked while Madelyn laughed at me. Some best friend she was.

"No." I shook my head. Using my fork, I blew on the sausage aggressively before taking a small bite. It was yummy.

"I'm tasty," Tom said. "I'm going to go get some drinks." He stood up from the bench. "You guys want some?" We all nodded.

"I'll go help," Daphne said, getting up. "I'm sure he can't carry them all by himself."

"Yeah," I said. "Please get me a bottle of coke and a straw. My tastebuds can't handle alcohol right now." Daphne nodded at me before disappearing into the cabin. As soon as Daphne left, Lily stood up, walked over to Anthony, and took Daphne's seat.

Anthony looked surprised by this. "Sorry," Lily said. "I wasn't comfortable over there. That chair is too hard. My buttocks hurt." Daphne's chair was the only one with a cushion while everyone else sat on hardwood. "Once she comes back, I'll return." When Tom and Daphne were back, Lily stood up immediately.

"No, it's fine," Daphne said. "You stay there." Lily sent her a grateful look and plumped back down.

Tom walked over to his wife. "Here," Tom handed her a drink, "I opened it for you already." I looked back at my drink. It still had its screw intact—no one to open drinks for me.

Well, isn't that so sweet of you, Tom.

"Thanks," Lily giggled. "I can't drink too much, though. Alcohol gets to me real fast." She sniffed the content first, squeezing her face at the odor that hit her nostrils. "Well, just for today," she said before she took a big gulp from the bottle.

"Woah, slow down," Anthony warned, patting her back softly. "You don't want to choke to death."

"Thank you," she said, laughing. "I think it went up my nose." It did go up her nose, dripping down. "Ewww," she said, collecting the tissue Anthony was already handing over to her.

The last time we decided to play a game, it didn't end well. This time Heather suggested Josh told the story of the time he got lost in Bangkok when chasing a Thai girl. I had heard the story a few times.

"Ewww," he said when Heather brought it up. "Please, I don't want to talk about it." But still, he went on to tell us how everything had happened. It wasn't long before someone else got our attention.

Lily wasn't wrong when she said alcohol got to her 'real fast.' In fact, it got to her a little too fast. Minutes later Lily was already drunk. She was laughing over anything that was said and was becoming all touchy with Anthony since he sat the closest to her. I looked at Tom, hoping he would go get his wife, but he didn't move.

"Lily, maybe you should have had a bottle of coke like Amelia," Heather said, her tone sounding worried. "The bottle is barely half empty, and you're already drunk." Heather looked back at Tom. I was hoping he would take this hint and go get his wife, but no, he still had his butt glued to his seat.

Lily gave Heather a sad pout. "Don't be a fun spoiler, Heather. I haven't even had one drink yet." She turned to Anthony, a cheeky smile on her face. "Do you want to have a sip from my drink? It's starting to taste funny." She held her bottle to his lips. "My tongue scratches."

Anthony chuckled, shaking his head. "No, thank you," he said. He looked to Daphne. His eyes seemed to be asking for help. "Maybe you've had enough?"

"Are you sure?" Lily's voice dropped even lower with each word. She moved closer. I sighed and braced myself for another fight. Tom finally got up from his seat and walked to his wife.

"Lily," he called. Just as the words left his lips, Lily slammed her lips against Anthony's. The Earth seemed to stop rotating for just a second, as we were all shocked at her action. Anthony's eyes were wide open, and it was apparent that even he didn't understand what had just happened.

The fight I had predicted finally popped up like Jack.

Chapter 14

Tom was the first to react. With a loud cry, he rushed toward Anthony. Lily, who had pulled back from the kiss, was giggling, not realizing the damage she had caused. The two men collided with great force, pushing themselves, a couple of chairs, and Lily to the ground.

"How dare you!" Tom shouted, delivering the first punch with his good arm. I looked at Josh, but he was already on his feet. From the way Tom delivered that first punch to Anthony's jaw, he had been waiting for a long time to do that. Tom and Anthony didn't get along. I hardly saw them in a conversation.

"Quit it, Tom." Josh tried to pull him back, but Anthony was already pushing Tom away. He was bigger, and from the looks of things, stronger.

"I'm not the one you should be angry at!" Anthony spat. "She's the one who kissed me, and you saw everything that happened. Why the hell are you coming at me?"

"How would you feel if I walked over to Daphne and kissed her? You didn't push her away or resist. You let her kiss you."

"I was taken aback, ok? I didn't expect it." Anthony's statement only seemed to anger Tom even more. He let out an angry growl trying to get out of Josh's stronghold. "I have a girlfriend. Why would I want to kiss your wife?" Anthony said.

"Ask yourself that question. You're the one who has been flirting with her ever since." Well, it's good that he wasn't blind, but then, Anthony hadn't been the one flirting. It had always been Lily.

"That's not true, and Lily is just teasing."

"You bastard. Let go of me, Josh! You enjoyed it, didn't you? You enjoyed the kiss, didn't you?"

"What are you even—you know what? Fine. Yes, I enjoyed the kiss. There is nothing I've wanted more on this trip than to kiss your wife. Her lips were so soft, and I would love to do it again!" I knew Anthony just said that to hurt Tom because he was angry, but I wished he would remember that his girlfriend was around and watching the whole drama.

"Tom, please calm down. It didn't mean anything," Lily cried. Daphne sat quietly as if she didn't know what to make of what happened. "He's right, and I'm the one at fault. I should have known better." Lily said.

When Tom seemed to have calmed down, Josh let go of him. He shot a look at Anthony as he walked to the cabin, slamming the door behind him hard.

Anthony finally remembered his girlfriend. He turned to Daphne, a sullen look on his face. "Daphne?" he called, but she paid him no attention. Not sparing him a glance, she stood up and walked to the cabin.

"Well, fuck my life," Anthony cussed. "I'm taking a walk down the river to clear my head." He grabbed the bottle of Vodka and walked into the darkness.

We watched him go until the trees blocked his path. "Well," Madelyn was the first to speak. "That's one way to throw a party. It's been long since I've watched such good drama." I shot her a look. It wasn't time for her sarcasm, but she didn't seem to care much. "Thanks a lot, Heather," she continued. "You really brought the fun."

Heather was about to speak when we got distracted by Lily's sobbing. She was sitting on the ground, with her hair in disarray, each strand pointing in a different direction. She hugged her knees, buried her head in between, and rocked herself slowly. I glanced at Madelyn, who shrugged, not knowing what to do.

"Lily," I walked toward her. "Are you OK?" She raised her head slowly to look at me. Her eyes were wide and scared. She muttered some inaudible words then went back to staring at the ground. "Lily?"

"I didn't mean it," I heard her say, in a tone too low. "I d—don't know what came over me," she stammered.

"I know," I said, bringing her into my arms. "You were under the influence—" she pushed me away, and before I could understand why, she was puking out everything she had downed. Luckily, she had acted quickly, and neither of us got stained. The stench hit my nose and seemed to affect a particular spot in my brain. I let out a small sneeze, fighting nausea that was rising already.

"I'm sorry," she said, wiping her mouth with her hands. "I shouldn't drink alcohol ever again. I barely had one bottle. It shouldn't have this much effect on me." She tried to get up. If I hadn't grabbed her fast enough, she would have lost her balance and landed on her vomit. "Thank you." She shot me a grateful smile. "Can you please help me to my room? I don't think I can make it on my own." I nodded, grabbing her arm and flinging it across my shoulders. Lily was a small woman and didn't weigh much.

A couple of candles illuminated the cabin. It was dark inside. Together we climbed up the stairs. Just as we were about to walk into her room, Tom came out. "I just came to grab a blanket. I will be sleeping on the couch downstairs tonight," he muttered, not looking at us. Without waiting for a response, he walked past us. Lily turned to grab his shirt, but I held her wrist, stopping her.

"Tom," she called weakly, but he didn't stop.

"Just let him go," I said. "He's angry. I'm sure by tomorrow, he will be calm, and you guys will work everything out." She nodded. We walked into the room, and I helped her into the bed. I was going to help her change into pajamas, but she said she was too tired.

"Amelia," she called me, her voice weak, her eyes closed.
"Yes?"
"They don't hate me, right?"
I frowned. "Of course not. Why will you even ask that?"

She smiled. "Because of what I did." Before I could speak, she asked, "Do you think I'm a bad person?"

"No, no. You are not a bad person," I said.

She opened her eyes slowly. I'm not sure if she could see my face because the flashlight was facing in a direction away from us, but she was watching me. She let out a sigh. "Thank you," she muttered. "Your words have made me feel better. I can sleep now." Before I could finish tucking her to the bed, she was asleep.

"Good night," I said.

The door opened, and Daphne walked in. "Daphne?" I was surprised to see her.

"I can't sleep with Anthony tonight. Since Tom is sleeping downstairs, I've decided to sleep here."

I looked from her to a sleeping Lily. "Are you sure? You know she didn't mean to kiss Anthony. She was—"

"I know," Daphne said. "I don't want to face Anthony when he comes back drunk." She looked at the open windows in the room. "I'm sure that's what he's doing, drinking."

"I'm sorry about earlier—"

Daphne gave a dry laugh. "Let's just move past today. I'm tired." I nodded and reached for my flashlight.

"Ok then, good night," I said, heading for the door.

"Night," she replied.

I went outside to meet with the guys. On the way, I passed Tom, who was already asleep on the couch in the living room.

Chapter 15

"How is she doing?" Madelyn asked after I sat on a bench.

"She's fine. She is sleeping already," I said.

"Daphne?" Heather asked.

"Eh...It's kinda weird, but she's with Lily," I told them.

"What? You left her with Lily?" Heather asked.

"Calm down. She's not angry with Lily, but she doesn't want to face Anthony. Lily is asleep already, so you don't have to worry about them getting in a fight. Besides, Daphne looks too tired to start a fight. I'm sure they will talk it over in the morning, and everything will be fine...I can't say the same about the boys, though."

Josh nodded. "Exactly. When Anthony and I were working on the kitchen window, he mentioned something like—"

"What?" Heather asked.

"He and Tom not getting along. He said Tom didn't have a problem with him before, but when he started dating Daphne and became friends with Lily, things changed." Josh shrugged. "It was obvious that Tom doesn't like Anthony because of Lily."

"It's his fault." I found myself saying.

"Why do you say that?" Madelyn asked.

"When we were coming back from the creek, I talked with Lily about her flirting with Anthony—"

"Wait, what?" Madelyn interrupted, laughing.

"I had to." I shrugged. "Anyways, she told me that Tom understood that the flirting was innocent and not to be taken seriously. She said Tom had said himself that he didn't mind."

"He didn't mind?" Heather repeated. "And she believed him? Oh, Lily can be so naive at times. But Tom should have laid down his feelings straight for her. If he didn't like it, then he should have come clean."

"Yeah," Josh said. "Yes, and if he had done that, I wouldn't have received the punch I got today." He frowned, touching an area at the corner of his lips.

"Sorry," Heather sympathized. "I wonder where Anthony is. I hope he's ok."

"He'll be fine," I assured her. "It's Anthony." I hadn't known him for long, but with the few days spent together, he had proven to be smart. "He wouldn't do anything stupid."

"Should we just leave them here and go home tomorrow?" Madelyn said.

I raised my hand immediately, and so did Josh. "You guys aren't serious, are you?" Heather asked. "I mean, we still have a few days here. We'd still enjoy our time."

"No offense Heather," Josh said. "But next time we plan to go on a trip, try not to like, let anyone in. Just to avoid situations like this."

"Yeah. I came here to have fun, not to listen to arguments and cries and watch relationships fall." I turned to Heather. "Thanks a lot. I'm having a great time."

"You're being sarcastic." Heather pouted and turned to me. "Sorry, Amelia. This isn't helping you forget about Ben, is it?"

Actually, at the moment, Ben was nowhere on my mind, not till she mentioned his name. I gave her a small smile. We were interrupted by a small creak that came from the door. It was Daphne. She had changed into her pajamas.

"Anthony isn't back?" Daphne asked.

"Not yet," Heather told her.

"Oh." She nodded her head. "Tom is sleeping in the living room. I'm going to be with Lily. She's in pretty bad shape." With that, she turned and walked back into the cabin.

"She would rather stay with Lily, who caused the fight?" Madelyn asked.

"Maybe she understands that Lily didn't mean to." Heather shrugged.

"Bullshit!" Madelyn spat. "Lily has done nothing but flirt with Anthony ever since we arrived here. She may have been under the influence of alcohol, but please, there was some part of her that must have wanted to kiss him."

"I agree," Josh said. "I can't wait to go back home. I feel like every time we settle a fight between them. Another one is already steaming, about to—" We heard approaching steps. It was Anthony, who had been gone for over an hour. I noticed something different. His breathing was loud and heavy, and his eyes were wild.

"Dude, are you ok?" Josh asked.

"I'm fine." He cleaned his mouth with the back of his hand. With staggering steps he proceeded to the cabin. His steps were so bad that I was worried he would fall. Josh moved to help him. "Don't touch me!" He shouted, waving Josh away. "I can walk on my own."

"Don't be stupid, dude. You're going to fall." Josh grabbed hold of his right arm, placing it over his shoulders. Anthony didn't push back this time. Not saying another word, he let Josh lead him into the house.

"Tomorrow morning, we will pack our things and leave," Madelyn was the first to break the air.

"Poor Anthony," Heather said. "He never liked alcohol. You know...after the incident."

"What incident?" I asked.

"Let's just say he drove around drunk one day and almost lost his life. He was an alcoholic then. He still drinks, but he's been trying to control it. He must be feeling terrible to get so drunk." Heather said.

"How long have they been dating?" I asked Heather.

"Daphne and Anthony? Just about three months. You know, it was Anthony who introduced me to them. He had a big crush on Daphne, but she rejected him till some months back, and they started dating."

"They are such a cute couple," Madelyn said. "Daphne is cool, and so is Anthony. They will solve the issue and get back together. It is just a matter of time. As for Lily and Tom? No offense, but their relationship is bound to crash." She went on to exaggerate her point by making an explosive sound.

"Don't say that. I'm sure they can work it out." I said, although I hardly believed it myself. I asked myself what they had seen in the other, seeing that they had no common interest and didn't agree on the same topic.

Madelyn scoffed, shaking her head. "I doubt it."

Heather gave a big yawn. "We should go inside and sleep. I'm tired of today." She stood up.

Madelyn also got up, following Heather. "I'm hungry." I heard her say. The barbecue she had prepared earlier was barely touched as everyone seemed to have lost appetite after the fight. "Amelia, aren't you coming?" Madelyn asked.

"Oh, I'm going to stay out for a while. I need to clear my head." Madelyn nodded, and they went inside.

I rested my head back, staring at the dark sky above. Little twinkling dots displayed all over. The brightest of them was the closest to the crescent-shaped silver moon. I remembered when I was little, whenever I saw a crescent moon, I would wonder who ate the other part of the moon. I thought we had different moons till I grew up and got to know better.

I took another sip of my Coke, but only air came up the straw. "Dang!" I might as well just go to sleep then. I looked at the mess around. No one would help me to clean it up, and I was exhausted. "Tomorrow, I guess."

I stood up and was surprised to see Daphne and Tom under a tree. They seemed to be involved in an important conversation. "I thought everyone had gone to sleep. What are you guys doing here?" I asked.

"Uh... I came to—"

"She came to give me my drugs," Tom completed for Daphne. "I still have a terrible headache." I nodded.

"I thought you had gone to bed," Daphne said. "I heard you guys came in."

"Oh, that was just Madelyn and Heather. I stayed out a little longer." We stared at each other in awkward silence. I cleared my throat. "Ok then, good night." I headed to the stairs.

"Night," Daphne said. "Amelia," she called my name, so I turned to face her. "Uh... That's not the direction to your room."

I was confused, and then I realized what she meant. I hurried down the stairs. "Silly me," I said. "The sleep is getting to me. Ok, later." I hurried to my room.

When I arrived, Heather and Madelyn were already asleep. I changed into my pajamas and climbed onto the bed, pushing away Madelyn, who had rolled to my side. After I laid down, Madelyn flung her arm to my cheeks, and one of her legs found its way to rest upon my stomach. I didn't even want to think of the position she lay in.

Sleep came almost immediately.

Chapter 16

I found myself sitting in a white office. There was a desk before me and a chair on the other side of the desk. A woman sat there. It was me. She was dressed in a black suit, her hair tied back in a tight bun. She had on glasses with rectangular frames. Her bright green eyes watched me like a hawk.

I'd been here before.

Placing her arms on the desk, she leaned forward. "So, why do you come here today?" Amelia asked me.

My session had begun.

"I think I finally know why Ben broke up with us." I didn't know why I said that.

She raised an eyebrow, leaning back to cross her legs. "Really? I see that your heart doesn't ache at the mention of his name. You've taken my advice?" She asked.

"Yes." I nodded.

"Good, so why do you think Ben broke up with us?"

"Because we are too amazing. He can't handle it?"

She threw her head back and laughed. "We both know that's a lie. Do you really know why Ben ended the nine-month relationship?"

I sighed. "Maybe it wasn't a matter of Ben and I not being perfect for each other. Maybe it's a matter of time."

She nodded her head. "Continue."

"Ben broke up with me because he wasn't ready. He was scared of the commitment."

"Good, now—"

The blood-curdling scream had me jump from the bed, my heart hammering hard against its cage. I wasn't sure if the scream came from my dream. It was weird that I had been speaking to myself.

I looked around the dark room, wondering if my mind was playing tricks with me. I lay still, waiting to hear the scream again. I reached out for Madelyn, who was still fast asleep. "Mads," I called, shaking her gently. When she didn't budge, I added a little force. "Madelyn, wake up!"

"You heard that too?" I almost screamed when I heard the question. A light struck my face, nearly blinding me. I closed my eyes, using my hands to block the light. "Sorry," Heather said. "Did you hear a scream?"

"Yes. You heard it too?" When the light was moved away, I opened my eyes and saw Heather sitting on her bed.

"Yes." She got out of bed. "It sounded like Daphne."

"Daphne? Did she have a bad dream?"

"She isn't with Anthony, right? I would think they got involved in a fight, but she's with Lily." Heather said. "And besides, Anthony loves Daphne. He would never hit her."

I looked toward our door. Silence was singing. "Should we go check up on her?" I asked.

"Do you think it's necessary?" Heather said. "It might—" The scream came again, this time even louder. "Ok, that's our answer. Wake Mads up. Let's go see what's wrong." At the sound of her name, Madelyn groaned loudly, rolling a bit toward me. She flung her hands, hitting me in the face.

"Hey," I rubbed the spot where she hit me. "Watch your hand. That was painful."

"Shut up," Madelyn said sleepily. "I'm trying to sleep. Shut up and go back to sleep. You two are making noise." She rolled back to her side, dragging my pillow along with her. She placed it over her head to block our voices.

"Madelyn," I called.

"Amelia, please, do not speak again. I'm having the most amazing dream ever. Chris Hemsworth and I are about to get married."

I rolled my eyes as I crawled over, dragging my pillow along with me. "Chris Hemsworth doesn't even know you exist."

"Fuck you," she muttered.

"Wake up. We have to check on Daphne." I got out of bed.

"Daphne, what happened to Daphne?" Madelyn finally sat up, rubbing her eyes. "Are they fighting again? Josh and Tom? Who is it this time?" she asked. "If they are, they should keep on fighting. Those two won't be the reason I don't marry Chris Hemsworth in my dream."

"I don't know if they are fighting," Heather said. She was already wearing her slippers. "Get up, Mads. Let's go make sure she's ok."

"If you two are so concerned, then go check on her yourself." She went back to sleep. "OK, you shouldn't bother. Do you still hear any scream?" There was nothing now. Everywhere was quiet, except our talks. "She probably got scared by a spider or cockroach, and Lily is with her, right?" Madelyn muttered into her pillows.

I looked at Heather. Madelyn was right. Lily was with Daphne, so... "Don't be lazy, Madelyn. What if those men who robbed us are back, and they are..." Heather said.

A terrible sight flashed between my eyes. It was this part that got Madelyn's attention.

"I'm only getting up because I don't want to be the reason that we don't get there in time to stop a murder or rape," Madelyn said.

Soon, we were out of the room, still in our pajamas and messy bedroom hair. With the aid of torchlight, we got through the dark house and started to climb the stairs. "Did you hear that?" Madelyn asked. "Someone's coming." We stopped in our steps to listen. Madelyn was right. Someone was approaching. "Quickly, off your light," she said. Heather and I turned off the torchlights, leaving us in darkness.

"What should we do?" Heather whispered. "The person is coming here."

I searched around and thanked the Lord when I touched a mop resting against the walls of the stairs. I had left the mop there after the cleaning earlier. "When the person gets here, we flash our lights to blind them, and I hit them with this mop," I said. "Then we call to the guys for help."

I held my breath as the steps got closer. "Now!" I shouted. We all turned on our flashlights. I gave a war cry and ran forward, ready to strike, but froze in my steps when I saw a familiar face. "Tom?"

"What are you doing here?" Heather asked. "We thought you were some intruder." She gave a nervous chuckle. "Sorry for the scare."

Tom looked surprised to see us. "I was sleeping in the living room. I came up to use the bathroom." He paused and wiped his wet hands on his clothes. "What's going on?"

Madelyn, Heather, and I glanced at each other. "We heard a scream," I told him. "We think it's Daphne."

"Daphne?" I could see his brows furrow as he asked. He looked in the direction of the room. Without another word, he hurried to the room. We followed quickly behind him. Tom pushed the door open, and we hurried inside.

Our lights first landed on Daphne. She sat on the floor beside the wardrobe, her knees to her chest. Tears were streaming down her pale face. "Daphne," Tom called. "What's wrong?" He asked.

"Lily," That was her response. She raised a shaky arm and pointed to the bed. Our eyes followed.

Heather was the first to scream. My entire body went numb, and I couldn't believe the sight before me. There on the bed, tucked almost in the same position I had placed her in, laid Lily, dead.

Chapter 17

"*But we only live this life once, and I can't take my money with me when I die. I've got to enjoy it while I'm still alive.*"

I wasn't sure how long we stood in a trance staring at Lily till Daphne jumped on her feet and raced to the bed. "I—I don't know what h—happened." Daphne's voice trembled. "Somebody... Oh my God! Lily!" She held Lily's arm, pulling and shaking. Judging by how badly Lily's throat was slashed, she was long gone.

"I'm still dreaming, right?" I heard Madelyn mutter. I also wanted to believe I was dreaming, but more than anything, I wanted to wake up. The whole sight before me was more terrifying than anything I've ever gone through.

"Don't just stand there!" Daphne shouted when she saw none of us had moved. "Do something!" She yelled. "Can't you see she's dying?"

Do something?

I didn't know what to do, how to think, and how to feel. My whole body went numb. How can Lily be dead? How can—

"Tom?" Daphne called, her voice shaky.

It was then that it hit me, Tom was there. I turned to look at him but couldn't see his face clearly. "Tom," I called his name softly. He turned to face me. "Tom. W—we will f—find whoever did this." I said. Tom took a step forward, then stumbled back, dropping down on his knees. He got up and ran to the bed.

"Guys, what happened? I heard someone scream," Josh said as he ran into the room. "Guys, what's going—what the fuck!" He shouted and ran forward to get a better view. He turned to look at me, Heather, and Madelyn, then back to the bed. "What happened? Why is there blood? What happened to Lily? Is this some kind of sick joke you guys are—" Tom's cries stopped him.

A clang was heard. Heather dropped her torchlight. Slowly, she walked toward the bed, kneeling beside Tom. She tried to place her arms on him, but he shrugged her hands away. Tearing his eyes from Lily, Tom faced Daphne. "What happened to Lily? What happened to my wife?"

I wanted to do something, to relieve Tom of the pain, to clean the tears rolling down Heather's cheeks, to bring Lily back. "I d—don't know, I woke up a—and saw this," Daphne said.

"I should have been here." Tom held on to Lily's gown, burying his face deep. "I should have been here with her. This wouldn't have happened if I were here."

"Can we call a doctor?" Daphne asked. "to save Lily?"

"It's too late, Daphne. Lily is already gone." I said.

There was a flushing sound that came from outside the room. Someone was in the toilet. "What's that?" Heather's head snapped to the door. "I heard something. Did you guys?" I nodded.

"S—someone is in the toilet," Madelyn stammered. "D—do you think it's..." She took a step away from the door.

The door to the toilet was opened and slammed shut. Heather let out a whimper. We moved away from the door, getting closer to the bed. Josh reached over for a stick nearby, holding it to his chest. We waited as the steps of the intruder got closer. I held my breath when I saw the intruder's shadow against the wall. It got smaller as the person got closer. I could hear the heavy breathing now.

"Fuck," I heard Madelyn mutter. "Is this how I die?" For a moment, I imagined the dead widow's son coming to kill all of us.

"Daphne." A voice called from outside the door. It was Anthony. I sighed in relief. "Please come back to the room," He said. "I'm sorry ok? It was stupid of me to...I shouldn't have let her, please."

"Anthony?" Madelyn called him. There was no response from the other side, and then slowly, Anthony came into the room. His eyes widened when he saw us, and he cleaned his mouth with the back of his palms.

"What's going on? What's everybody doing here? Where's Daphne—" His eyes traveled to the bed. "Lily?"

"Lily is dead," Madelyn told him.

"W—what h—how is that p—possible..." He ran toward the bed. Tom was quick to get on his feet, pushing Anthony back.

"Don't you dare touch her!" He yelled. "This is all your fault! If you hadn't kissed my wife, I would have been here. I could have prevented it." He turned back to face Lily and caressed her face. "Lily should be alive."

"Guys, we have to find out who did this. This isn't the time to accustom blame to anyone." I said. The fact that a murderer was still around the cabin or probably in the same room with me was utterly terrifying. My body shook frantically as we all stood in silence. Tom was crying while Daphne comforted him.

Daphne.

Did she kill Lily? Because of the kiss earlier? Daphne was such a sweetheart. She wouldn't have the heart to do something like that, but then you could tell a person by their appearance. Daphne had been in the room with Lily and could have done it. But she looked genuinely heartbroken, and it's hard to picture her being the killer.

"We need to call the cops," Josh broke the silence. "The murderer could not have gotten far, or worse—" he looked toward Daphne, taking a slight pause. "Still with us."

Anthony noticed this. "Why the fuck are you looking at her?" He asked, taking a step toward Josh. "If you're thinking—"

"Calm down, Anthony," Madelyn was quick to say. "Now isn't the time to fight. Josh isn't insinuating anything. We just have to think." She looked at me. I could tell Madelyn was trying to be strong. Her voice was hoarse as if it pained her to speak. "Amelia, you're a detective. What should we do?"

I gulped audibly as everyone turned to look at me. I was no detective. Madelyn liked to call me that because I was a keen observer. Taking a deep breath, I tried to steady myself.

I opened my mouth to speak but found no words. They were all waiting for me to speak. I knew we were in a tight spot, and someone had to step up to the plate. I cleared my throat, then said, "Josh, you call the cops. Tell them a murder has taken place and give them the location." He nodded, moving out of the room.

"What do we do?" Heather asked, turning to glance at Lily's corpse again. She looked away quickly. "Please say something Amelia, I'm scared. I can't be here anymore. I don't want to die..."

"Hey," Madelyn brought her in for a hug. "You're not going to die. We're going to find the monster who did this." Heather sniffed, not saying anything.

"We search to see if the murderer is still hiding inside the house. We have to be careful. For all we know, the murderer could still be nearby," I said the last part slowly, watching everybody's faces. I didn't add the part that the murderer could be among us. Before I left the room, I stepped closer and forced myself to take a careful look at Lily's corpse, especially the slash on her neck. The cut looked deeper at the right side of her neck, showing that's where the knife was placed to slice through.

Lily had a peaceful look on her face, just the way she had been when I tucked her in earlier. Tears stung at my eyes, and words couldn't even describe the emotions running through me. I remembered the way her eyes would crinkle with excitement as she told everyone the stories of her honeymoon, her laugh that always brightened the room, and her love for adventure. If I could bring Lily back, I would take her to the zoo and see a bear. I tore my eyes away from her. "Let's search the house first."

"I'll stay here with Tom," Daphne said.

Minutes later, we each held a torchlight. We formed two teams as it was not a good idea to be alone. Josh, Heather, and Anthony went outside to check. Madelyn and I started searching the rooms. Madelyn held tight to a knife she got from the kitchen while I held on to a hammer.

"This is crazy," I heard her mutter. "I want to leave this place now and never return." We slowly approached the room where Anthony and Daphne were sleeping in. Madelyn pushed open the door with her feet and moved aside for me to take the first step in. "Ladies first," she said.

"We're both 'ladies,' Madelyn."

"Fine. But you're going in first, Amelia."

I shook my head and walked in. There was no time to argue. We looked at every corner of the room, under the bed, in the wardrobe, behind the curtains, but there was nothing. "Let's go," Madeline said, standing by the bed. "I wish the cops would arrive here fast. I'm scared." She picked up a pillow from the bed and flung it across the room with a frustrated sigh.

When the pillows landed, I heard a sound, a sound you would get if you scraped your spoon against the tiles. "Did you hear that?" I walked toward the pillow.

Madelyn looked at me, confused. "Hear what? I didn't hear anything. Did you hear something?" She flashed her light around the room.

"When you threw the pillow..." I walked over and kneeled before the pillow. "I thought I heard... Yes. I did hear something."

"Like what?" She asked, suddenly very nervous. I picked up the pillow, turning it around. "Fuck!" Madelyn shouted, making me jump. "Is that blood?"

Not only was the pillow stained with blood, but there was an object inside. It was shaped like a knife. Quickly, I dragged the pillow cover out. There laid Josh's knife, the gold knife he found days ago by the river.

"Isn't that Josh's knife?" Madelyn asked. "What's it doing in Anthony's and Daphne's room?"

I looked at her. "Madelyn, Daphne wasn't here. It was just Anthony." I looked back at the knife. "Does that mean—"

"A—Anthony killed Lily?"

Chapter 18

"We have to let the guys know." Before I could utter another word, Madelyn rushed out of the room. I stood lost for a moment before following her. "Josh!" She shouted. "Josh!" We hurried down the stairs, running outside to warn him. The front door was opened just as we reached the foot of the stairs.

"What's wrong?" Josh ran inside with Heather and Anthony. "Did you find something?" They were drenched from head to toe. It was only when the thunder roared that I realized it was raining. "Anything? I heard you call my name."

"He killed Lily!" Madelyn shouted, pointing at Anthony. "He is the one who killed Lily!"

"What?" Heather said in a raised voice. She looked at Anthony and then back to Madelyn. Anthony looked stunned by the accusation. "Madelyn, I think you should drop down those accusing fingers."

"You killed her, you bastard! We found the knife in your room. Don't act like you don't know what I'm talking about." Madelyn shouted.

Anthony raised an eyebrow. "What knife? What are you saying?" He looked at me. "What's going on, Amelia? Has your friend gone nuts? I know we're all losing it after—"

"I said don't act like you don't know what I'm talking about, you murderer!" With lightning speed, Madelyn threw her slippers at him. Anthony dodged, and the slippers hit the door behind him. Madelyn moved forward, but Josh grabbed her before she could strike Anthony. Josh had been the one separating all the fights that had risen. I wondered what would have happened if he wasn't around.

"Calm down, Mads," Josh said, holding tight to a struggling Madelyn. "Amelia, please explain."

"Madelyn and I searched the room Anthony lay with Daphne. There we saw your knife, Josh. The one you found by the river. It was coated with blood. No question, it was Lily's blood," I said, looking at Anthony to see his reaction. He looked lost, like a deer caught in headlights.

"What the fuck are you saying?" Anthony scoffed. "I have never even touched Josh's knife. Why would I even—you are making no sense, is this some ploy?"

"This is no ploy, Anthony," I raised my flashlight to him, looking at his clothing. If he was the one who killed Lily, maybe—and I saw exactly what I didn't want to see. I don't know why no one noticed it before. We were probably too shocked even to notice. "Blood? Is that blood on your shirt?"

Anthony looked down to where the flashlights were pointed because everyone had turned theirs on him. There, just at the hem of his shirt were bloodstains, and I could see stains on his jeans too. Heather let out a scream running away from him. "Anthony, what the fuck?" That was the first time I'd heard Heather swear.

Anthony looked stunned. "W—what is... I don't know how this... This doesn't make sense!" He shouted, looking up at us. "I didn't kill Lily. You have to believe me." His eyebrows were furrowed, his face set in a frown. I could see the fear in his eyes, mixed with panic. "I don't know what this is."

"You were pretty drunk last night," I jumped as I heard Daphne's voice from behind. Behind Daphne was a distressed-looking Tom, who held onto her hand. Together, they walked into the living room.

"Daphne," Anthony called softly. He tried to walk to her but stopped when she took a cautious step back.

"Don't come close to me," Daphne said. She had stopped crying. "I heard everything. Now that I think of it, the silhouette I had seen in the room fit your exact psychic. You do terrible things when you are drunk, Anthony." By the time she called his name, fresh tears were rolling down.

Tom took a step forward, his eyes on Anthony. "Why?" He asked, though no words came out. I had just read his lips.

"I didn't kill Lily!" Anthony gave a crazed laugh. "Fuck, I didn't get that drunk—" Taking everyone by surprise with speed, Tom rushed forward, head-butting him to the floor. They crashed down together, knocking over a chair nearby. Anthony let out a loud grunt as his back landed on the hard floor.

"Get off me!" He shouted, trying to push Tom away. Though Anthony might have been stronger, Tom was angrier.

"I swear I'll kill you," Tom yelled, holding tight to Anthony's throat. "What did she do to you?" He added pressure to his hold with each word, squeezing hard. Anthony started to choke.

"Please," Daphne sobbed. I walked over to her, taking her into my arms to comfort her. She threw her head on my shoulders, sobbing. "Lily wasn't the kindest soul, but she was trying. What would he gain from killing her," she cried. That was the question I had been asking myself, what would Anthony gain from killing Lily? In all the ways I've looked at it, nothing—except a sick satisfaction I would never understand. He—

I was brought out of my thoughts by the sounds of the sirens approaching. Josh tried to separate the two men. "Don't do anything stupid, Tom! You kill him, and you end up in jail. Let the cops take care of this."

"I don't care!" Tom shouted. "I will go to jail as long as he's dead."

"The cops are here. They will take care of him!" Josh shouted as he struggled to hold on tight to Tom. Josh was big compared to Tom, a small man, so it would be easy to control him on an average day, but this wasn't Tom on an average day. He had just lost his wife.

Heather was crying now, and so was Madelyn. I couldn't cry, I was thinking. I had to think, for Lily.

"Get the fuck away from me!" Tom swung around, landing a punch straight to Josh's chin. "Fuck," Tom moaned in pain as he had used his bad arm. This weakened the hold Tom had on Anthony, enabling Anthony to push Tom away.

I could hear the sirens clearly now. The cops had arrived. Daphne was crying harder, her shoulders shaking with each sob. Heather moved closer to comfort her. But I still couldn't wrap my head around the whole thing. I jumped when I felt Madelyn's hands around mine. The four of us were together, watching the boys.

"You are crazy!" Anthony choked out once Tom was pulled off him. "I didn't kill Lily!" He turned to a crying Daphne, who turned her face away the moment his eyes met hers. "You have to believe. I would never do—" He stopped when she didn't face or answer him. "Seriously?" He was angry now. "Fuck you! What happened to trust? How do you think I'll ever do something like that?"

"Please, Anthony!" Daphne shouted, surprising me. I had never seen her voice raised to such a tone. "All evidence points at you. What was the knife doing in your pillow?"

Two cops walked in at that moment, kicking the door open as they stormed in. They stopped when they saw us. "We got a call," the older cop said, stepping forward.

"He killed my wife!" Tom yelled, pointing at Anthony. "He killed Lily!" He cried.

"I didn't!" Anthony shouted. "Stop saying that. I was drunk, but I wasn't so drunk that I wouldn't know my actions!" He turned to Heather. "Please, not you too."

"Motherfucker! I'll kill you!" Tom pushed Josh away and rushed toward Anthony again, but the younger cop stopped him.

"It's ok now," the officer grabbed Tom's left arm and pulled him back. "We'll take it from here."

"This is Tom's strength. He's left-handed, you know, which is good for him because Tom's right hand is still weak because of the accident."

Lily had said these words yesterday morning at the creek. "Wait!" I found myself saying.

Chapter 19

Money, they said, is the root of all evil. The whole trip, from the time we stepped our feet in the cabin to this moment, replayed in my head—every action, every conversation, every fight, and Lily. Lily came to my mind.

Everyone in the room, including Anthony, looked at me. "What do you mean by that, Miss?" The older cop asked. He already had his cuffs out for Anthony, but now it dangled from his hand.

In my mind, everything fell into place, and I had a crazy theory. If I were correct, then... I turned to face Daphne and took a step away from her. "How did you know?" I asked.

"Know what?" Daphne cleaned her eyes, sniffing. "What are you saying?" The more I thought about it, the more I believed I was right. Now I knew why she hadn't defended Anthony and didn't care to hear from his side. She was quick to accuse him of killing Lily.

"Earlier, you asked Anthony, 'What was the knife doing in your pillow?' It just hit me... Madelyn and I never mentioned where we found the knife. How did you know the knife was in the pillow?" Her eyes widened. She glanced at Tom, then back at me. She opened her mouth to speak, but no words came out.

"What's with this stupid question?" Tom asked angrily. "We already know who killed my wife, enough of this nonsense."

"I know you're going through pain. We all are, but let her speak." Madelyn turned to me. "Amelia, what's wrong?" She asked.

I twisted my palms into angry fists. Every second that passed, more clues ticked in place. "T—Tom and Daphne were the ones that brought us the drinks at the barbecue last night. All our bottle caps were still in place, except Lily's. Remember?" I turned to Josh. I'm not sure if he remembered, but he nodded. "That's because Tom had opened Lily's bottle and put something inside. Right?" I turned to Tom. "You put something inside Lily's drink. She had just one bottle, just like the rest of us, yet she acted like she was under the influence of a drug."

"Watch your mouth, Amelia," Tom warned, taking a threatening step toward me, but the younger officer stopped him. "Are you saying that I would drug my wife?"

"Let the woman speak," the officer said to Tom, then looked at me. "Go on."

"The other day," I turned to Heather. "We were both here in the living room while the others had gone to the river, remember?" Heather nodded her head quickly. "We saw Daphne, and she went to check up on Tom to give him his drugs. Last night," I turned to Daphne, who was looking at me with an unreadable expression on her face. "when I had walked in on you, you two were discussing how to kill Lily, right?" Daphne avoided my eyes.

A rage soared through my body, and I raised my voice. "You were the one who suggested the barbecue, and you were the one who gave Lily the drink. You both planned this from the start. What did you put into Lily's drink?"

The room became silent. Everyone was stunned, except the police and me. I was furious and shaking.

"You're saying nonsense, Amelia," Daphne said. "Just because I suggested the barbecue and bought Tom Tylenol? If someone else had done this, would you be questioning them?"

"You still haven't answered her question," Josh said. "How did you know they found the knife in Anthony's pillow?" He asked. Daphne fell quiet. I could see from her eyes that she started to panic. I just needed to push a little more, and the truth would come out.

"The reason you chose to sleep with Lily last night wasn't that you couldn't bear to face Anthony," I continued. "It was to clear your name off the chart. Because then we wouldn't pin the murder on you. Here is what I think really happened." I faced the cops. "Tom killed Lily, and Daphne helped hide the murder weapon in Anthony's pillowcase. What did you both stand to gain? All of Lily's wealth."

"Bitch!" Daphne screamed, running toward me. Before I could react, a slap landed on my face. The force almost knocked me off balance. I caught myself with the aid of the chair behind me. "How dare you!" She scratched at my face, but Madelyn pushed her away.

Tom was already fidgeting. "It's not true. All she's saying is a lie. I l—loved my wife."

"Here's how I knew you were the one who killed Lily." The look on his face scared me. I was afraid anytime soon he would run across the room to me, but the young officer stepped in front of me. "The slash on her throat was deeper from the right side of her neck, moving on to the left. The killer would have to do this with his left hand. You're left-handed, Tom."

"That proves nothing!" He shouted. "Anyone could easily have used their left hand. I was asleep in the living room."

"Well, I can see you've changed your clothes." He looked down at his clothes, then back at me. "Why did you change clothes? You were sleeping in the living room hours ago with the clothes you wore in the day. You couldn't have gotten a change of wear unless you entered the room where your clothes are, and that's in Lily's room."

He gave a dry laugh, which reminded me of the one Daphne gave when I left her in the room with Lily. "You're crazy," Tom said. "Are you even listening to yourself? I'm the murderer because I changed my clothes?"

I ignored him and continued. "When you were coming from the bathroom, you had just finished washing up. Am I right? That's after Daphne had placed the murder weapon in Josh's pillow and returned to the room."

"Bitch!" Daphne shouted, trying to fight the strong hold of the officer. "I never liked you! Any of you!"

"This doesn't make sense. She's just spitting rubbish. I would never hurt Lily. She's my wife. Ok? I loved her," Tom said to the officers. "Surely you don't believe this crazy woman."

"I am listening. " The older officer said.

"You and Daphne were always close. Daphne had introduced you to Lily together because of her wealth. This has been your plan for how many years?" Heather asked. "And with Lily dead, as her husband, you earn everything."

"I bet you, if we search around a little, we'll find the drugs you used. We could take it to the lab to find out what kind of drugs they are," Madelyn added. "I bet they aren't painkillers."

"It was all his idea!" Daphne suddenly shouted, surprising everyone. "I never wanted my hands stained. He pushed me."

"Shut up! You were the one who introduced Lily to me. This was your plan all along." Tom shot back.

"Well, I told you to wait, didn't I?" Daphne yelled. "After the joint account, you were supposed to be patient and wait. Now I'm going to jail because of you."

"Fuck you! If you hadn't opened your big mouth, our plan would have worked. And he!" He tried to point at Anthony, but the cops were holding his hands tight. "He should be the one going to jail."

Honestly, I didn't think that would be possible. They had made so many silly mistakes. It was just a matter of time before it was revealed that Anthony was innocent and they were the real murderers.

"Ok, we've heard enough," The older officer said. "You two are coming with us to the station."

"Yes, take them already," Madelyn said. "You guys are going to rot, and Tom, I pray your ass tears when those prisoners work on you."

"No!" Daphne cried as she was put in cuffs. "I can't go to prison. Anthony, please do something!" Daphne pleaded. Anthony didn't say a word or move an inch. "Anthony!" She called again. When he turned his head away from her, Daphne got violent. "Bastard! I hate you! I never loved you, ok? Bastard!" She was acting like a crazed woman now, cursing, kicking, scratching, trying to break free from the officer's hold. She was dragged out along with a crying Tom. Tom didn't put up any resistance, just allowed the cops.

A few minutes later, a forensic team arrived. When Lily's corpse was carried out, I saw her face again in the dim light. She still had that same peaceful look. Maybe she found peace on the other side.

Chapter 20

We followed the cops to the station to drop our statements. We were held at the station while the forensic team swept the cabin for evidence. Hours later, a cop came to the room we were in, telling us that we were free to go but could be contacted later for more info.

We drove back to the cabin to pack our things. The morning had arrived, and I could see the sun rising from the east. It reminded me of the first morning here in this woods—Earth was alive. The joyous vibe the morning brought contrasted with the horrors of the night. It was a painful reminder that the world doesn't stop just because your heart does. The people will grieve for weeks or months, but that's all. The world moves on while the ones who have kissed the dust are left behind. I wept for Lily.

We didn't say one word to each other all the way back. I sighed when the cabin came into view. The feeling of déjà vu rose.

"Well," Josh said as he turned off the ignition. "Let's pack and get the hell out of here. I never want to step foot into this woods again."

"Yeah, let's hurry and leave," Heather said.

I shoved my clothes into my bags, not caring to arrange them. Then I moved on to my books, which I hadn't gotten the time to read—except the one with the thirteenth-century soldier.

"Look," Madelyn said, pointing at an object on the floor. She bent to pick it up. "It's the necklace Lily gave me." She showed it to Heather and me. "I don't think I should take it. I'll leave it here." Looking up at us, she asked, "Or what do you guys think?"

I didn't know what to say. "You could keep it," Heather told her. "For Lily."

We went back to our clothes, leaving Madelyn to decide. Once we were done, we left the keys on the door.

"Josh?" Heather knocked on his door. "Are you ready?"

"We're in here!" Josh shouted from upstairs. He must be with Anthony. We walked up the stairs. A cold chill ran through my spine as we passed Lily's room. For some strange reason, I felt if we walked into the room, we would see Lily, smiling and waving at us. We hurried past to Anthony's room. The door was wide open.

Anthony sat on the bed, staring off into space. Though Anthony was a big man, he now looked small and drained. Gone was the man who was shot out of a Harlequin novel. His eyes carried heavy bags, and his hair was in disarray. "What's going on?" Madelyn asked.

Josh, who was shoving clothes into a bag, stopped what he was doing to answer. "I'm helping Anthony pack. He's not really in the right—"

"Let's just leave it," Anthony said, pushing away the clothes that Josh had gathered. "Let's go home." He let out a shaky breath.

Anthony had just lost a friend and partner. Now that I looked at it again, Lily had been the closest to Anthony. She had made him laugh in ways I never saw Daphne did. Daphne, the woman he had been in love with, didn't love him at all.

"Let's just go," Anthony said. "Josh, leave the bag. I don't need anything from here."

On our way home, we saw the haunted house Josh said belonged to the widow. When I sat up to take a closer look, I saw the two men who had broken into our cabin. It was only after we entered the highway that I closed my eyes to sleep.

Chapter 21

Dear Diary,
It's been two weeks since Lily's murder. Tom and Daphne were still in police custody, and tomorrow will be their first appearance in court.

We are still recovering from Lily's death. I hope she's in a happy place, far away from the evil the world holds.

"I know it's been two weeks already, but Lily's death still holds me by the throat." Heather sighed. "I can't believe I had dined and partied with these people, not knowing they were capable of committing murder, and I had invited them to the trip with us."

Since the horror in the woods, everyone had recoiled back to their rooms. This was the first time we met at the café.

"You couldn't have known, Heather," Josh said. "We also dined with them, and their wicked goals were not written on their foreheads. Also, do you know how long they've been planning that? If it weren't in the woods, they would have found another time to murder Lily."

"Yeah," I agreed. "How about we just forget about this and move on?"

"The court hearing is tomorrow, right?" Madelyn asked, rubbing her forehead. "There is too much in my head. I'm forgetting a lot."

"Yes," Heather replied.

"Good, I can't wait. I want to see their faces when they realize that the rest of their lives will be spent in prison, and they are begging for mercy. Josh, you said you wouldn't be able to make it." Madelyn said.

Josh shook his head. "No, I can't. I've got an important exam tomorrow. Professor Jones always picks the wrong time...It sucks. I really wanted to be there."

"Don't worry," Heather said. "I'll tell you everything." She looked at me. "Amelia, I saw Ben on my way here. He uhm...he asked of you."

"Oh, ok," I said.

Madelyn gave me a side look. "So?"

"So?" I questioned back.

"You're not going to call him? To talk?"

"Why should she?" Josh said. "If he wants to see her, he knows where she lives. He can call if he wants to talk."

"Yeah." Heather nodded. "But—" she turned to me, "Didn't he call you already, and you didn't pick up?"

"Let's not talk about Ben," I said.

"Right. Let's forget about Ben," Madelyn said. "Amelia has gotten over Ben."

"We should be looking more at setting her up with a new guy," Heather said. I raised an eyebrow at that. I didn't want a new guy. I wanted no guy. In fact, after the whole cabin trip, a relationship is the last thing I want to get myself involved in.

"Exactly." Madelyn snapped her fingers. "A friend of mine is currently on the road, and I could introduce you two together." She smirked in my direction. "Remember Kelvin from the drama club?" I remembered Kelvin. How could I forget the guy who had kept on staring at my breast when I went to buy tickets for the play Madelyn auditioned for?

"No, thank you," I said. "I'm not looking for a relationship, and even if I were, Kelvin would be the last person on my mind. Also, next time you see him, tell him he should learn to look at people's faces when he speaks to them and not their chest."

"Oh yeah, he said to apologize for that. Apparently, you had given him one or two words." Madelyn said. "But if you don't want Kelvin, what about Eric?"

"Who is Eric?" Heather asked.

"He's also in the drama club, and he's really cute," Madelyn told Heather. "And single," she added.

"Wait a minute." Josh threw his head back, laughing. "Didn't you get kicked out from the drama club because you were...Sorry, you *are* a terrible actress?"

"Fuck you, Josh!" Madelyn snapped. "It's not my fault those people don't know how to appreciate real talent."

"Don't know how to appreciate true talent? I think they will when they see one."

"What do you even know, your tits for brain...?"

It was nice to see the group being normal again. By normal, I meant destructive. I missed moments like this. It'd been long since I saw a smile on anyone's face. Heather and I watched silently as Madelyn and Josh continued to fight.

Chapter 22

Dear Diary,
It's been a while, right?
Yesterday, Lily was finally put to rest. After the court sentence that took place last week, Tom and Daphne were put behind bars for a long time. Tom had confessed to the whole crime and Daphne as his accomplice.

According to Tom, the whole thing was planned. They had been following Lily around. When Daphne found the Yoga class Lily attended, she signed up too. This was to befriend Lily and get her to Tom. It was easy for them because Lily was lonely and didn't have many friends. Also, it turned out the reason Tom hated Anthony wasn't because of Lily but Daphne. Tom and Daphne were in a secret relationship. Daphne had only gotten into a relationship with Anthony so that Lily wouldn't question her relationship with Tom.

Their original plan was to kill and dump Lily in the woods. It could be that Lily sensed something or just her survival instinct, that she sought the company of Anthony and never left the group. As the trip was coming close to an end and their time was running *out, it was their desperate gamble to murder Lily when she was asleep and framed it on Anthony.*

Lily's parents are still heartbroken over her death. The guys and I went to see them last week and again yesterday after Lily's burial to comfort them. We informed them about the candle night we were holding for Lily. I feel very sorry for them because they have no other child. Heather had promised Mrs. Clinton, Lily's mom, that she would always be there for her as a daughter.

Anthony is doing well now. He moved on from Daphne and said he wouldn't allow a monster to bring him sleepless nights. This evening, we will hold a candle night for Lily to pray for her soul and happiness in the afterlife.

The evening sky was clear. A full moon proudly sat in the sky, the stars twinkling around. "I'm nervous," Heather said as we watched the gathering crowd from the back of the stage. "I don't know what to say, Amelia." She let out a loud sigh.

"Heather, you're going to be fine," I assured her.

She shook her head. "No, no, Amelia. I've never been to something like this before. What speech should I deliver? What if I say something wrong? I want this to go on well. It has to, for Lily." I had just dried her tears a few minutes ago, but it looked like she was about to cry again.

I held her by the shoulders, trying to calm her. "Calm down. If you start thinking about it too much, I'm afraid you're going to have a panic attack." Her eyes widened at that, and her breathing seemed to have gotten heavier because of my words. "Just...just say what you feel, you don't have to make it perfect, you just go out there and let them...let them know who Lily was. Just tell them about the Lily you knew." When I finished, she didn't say a word, just kept on staring at me. "Heather?"

She blinked. "Yeah?"

"Did you hear what I just said?"

She nodded. "Yes, yes, thank you." She gave a small smile. "Ok." She gave a small sniff. "I should say whatever I feel, right?" I nodded. "Whatever I feel," she muttered under her breath.

I turned to look at who was coming when I heard steps approaching. It was Madelyn. "Heather, are you ready? It's time. People are waiting."

"Ok, give me one moment, and I'll be out," she said. Madelyn nodded and walked away. "You should follow her," Heather said to me. "I'll be out in a minute."

I gave her a pat on the back and went to find the guys. But they found me first, waving me over. "Hey, is Anthony here yet?" I asked.

"No," Josh answered. "But he said he was going to be here."

We waited for Heather while the lighting of the candle was going on. I spotted Lily's parents. I was glad they had shown up. Mrs. Clinton held on tight to her husband.

"Here," Madelyn said, bringing her candle that was already lit to touch the thread of mine.

"Thank you," I said. I turned to help the next person. It was Anthony. I didn't know when he had arrived. He brought his candle close, and we repeated the ritual. Then he turned to help the next person. "You made it," I whispered to Anthony.

"I wouldn't miss it," He said. "Knowing Lily, if I dared miss an event like this, she would haunt me forever." I smiled at that, knowing he was only just joking. Though it had me wondering, was it possible that Lily would be here today, watching us?

When everyone had their candles lit, Heather climbed the stairs to the stage where everyone could see her.

"Is she ok?" Madelyn whispered to me. "She doesn't look too good."

Heather looked nervous, but her hands weren't shaking as badly as before. "She will be fine," I said.

It took time before Heather started to speak. "Good evening, everyone. Thank you all for coming," she began. "My name is Heather Gilbert, and I was a friend of Lily's..." She paused her eyes, searching the crowd, till she found us. I gave her an encouraging smile. "I didn't come up here with a prepared speech," Heather continued. "I didn't come here to paint Lily with perfectness. I wouldn't say I had the best friendship with her because I didn't have enough time to really get to know her. If there was one thing I learned from Lily, it was to chase true happiness and not just material things. Lily never cared for those things, and she wanted companionship, love, and friends. I met Lily through a friend of mine, and even after I had known her for months, we didn't really get to talking till her last days on Earth. I remember her laughs. I'm happy that she..." She stopped to wipe at the tears that were rolling down her cheeks. "She was laughing. I'm happy that I saw her happy, and I wish I had the chance to know her more so I could have been there for her when she was at her lowest. She was a positive thinker, one of the brightest people you'll ever come across, and oh, she did have her crazy side." Heather gave a little laugh. She took a deep breath, breathing out slowly. "She...she wasn't a perfect person. But believe me, she was trying. I know if Lily were here today, she wouldn't want people crying for her because she's in a better place." The session ended with Heather leading us in prayer. "Lord, we are gathered here tonight because our loved one has departed from this Earth..." After the prayer session, a photo of Lily was raised while everyone looked up at it. "In the silence of our heart, let us all pray that Lily finds peace."

I had only known Lily for two weeks. I'd never heard of her in school and never seen her until Heather introduced us together. Never did I think she would have such an impact on me. Lily had been all in for happiness. She never had that many people around her. The people she had wanted to be friends with were after her money. It was funny because the first time I met her, I kind of envied her, the places she had been, the things she owned...I felt bad for that now.

I wished I had known Lily earlier, and I wished I was the one she had met at the Yoga class. Then I would befriend her, and I would introduce her to true friendship. She would be alive and happy, and meet people that would love her for who she truly was.

The candle night stayed for an hour in total silence, praying that Lily found happiness in the afterlife.

***

"Thank you so much," Mrs. Clinton said to Heather for the umpteenth time. "Though this wouldn't bring my Lily back, your kind words and the idea of organizing this touched us. Seeing the people who had gathered here for Lily lightens the pain in my heart. Thank you."

"It's nothing, Mrs. Clinton," Heather told her and leaned toward her for another hug. The two of them had become close over the past week. I was blessed the day I ran into Heather here at Stanford. She had the kindest soul ever.

"Miss Amelia Duke," Mr. Clinton said to me. "I would never be able to thank you enough for helping catch those monsters."

"You are welcome, sir. I'm just happy that I thought fast enough and that they are in prison, right where they belong." I said.

"If you need anything." He reached into his pockets and brought out a card. "Just reach out to me."

I nodded, taking the card. "Thank you."

"You did great out there, Heather," Josh said. "If Lily was here, I'm sure she would tell you so herself."

"Thanks, Josh," Heather said. "I'm just glad it went smoothly." She gave a slight cough, clearing her throat. "Say, how about we go to the cafe and grab some coffee to end the day." My throat suddenly felt scratchy as she said that.

"Sure," Madelyn said.

"Yeah. I could also have some fried chicken," I said, rubbing my stomach.

Together, we left the assembly ground.

www.ingramcontent.com/pod-product-compliance
Lightning Source LLC
LaVergne TN
LVHW041708060526
838201LV00043B/638